Dedalus Afric
General Edit

Yovanka Perdigão

TCHANAZE

CARLOS PARADONA RUFINO ROQUE

TCHANAZE

Beauty and the Beads

translated by
Jethro Soutar & Sandra Tamele

Dedalus

This book has been selected to receive financial assistance from English PEN's "PEN translates" programme, supported by Arts Council England. English PEN exists to promote literature and our understanding of it, to uphold writers' freedoms around the world, to campaign against the persecution and imprisonment of writers for stating their views, and to promote the friendly co-operation of writers and the exchange of ideas.

With support from Camões I.P. and the DGLAB/Cultura – PORTUGAL

Published in the UK by Dedalus Limited
24-26 St Judith's Lane, Sawtry, Cambs, PE28 5XE
info@dedalusbooks.com
www.dedalusbooks.com

ISBN printed book 978 1 915568 26 7
ISBN ebook 978 1 915568 66 3

Dedalus is distributed in the USA & Canada by SCB Distributors
15608 South New Century Drive, Gardena, CA 90248
info@scbdistributors.com www.scbdistributors.com

Dedalus is distributed in Australia by Peribo Pty Ltd
58, Beaumont Road, Mount Kuring-gai, N.S.W. 2080
info@peribo.com.au www.peribo.com.au

First published by Dedalus in 2024

Printed and bound in the UK by Clays Elcograf S.p.A.
Typeset by Marie Lane

THE AUTHOR

CARLOS PARADONA RUFINO ROQUE

Carlos Paradona Rufino Roque was born in 1963 in Inhaminga, Mozambique. He has worked as a lawyer, a social sciences researcher and a journalist.

He has three novels to his name: *Tchanaze, a donzela de Sena* (*Tchanaze*, 2009), *N'tsai Tchassassa, a virgem de missangas* (*N'tsai Tchassassa, Virgin of the Beads*, 2013), *Carota N'tchakatcha, feitiços e mitos* (*Carota N'tchakatcha, Spells and Myths*, 2018). He has also written a collection of poems: *A Gestação do Luar* (*The Moon's Gestation*, 1991).

He is the current Secretary General of the Association of Mozambican Writers.

THE TRANSLATORS

JETHRO SOUTAR

Jethro Soutar is a translator of Spanish and Portuguese. He is the general editor of the Dedalus Africa list and has translated *The Ultimate Tragedy* by Abdulai Silá and *The Madwoman of Serrano* by Dina Salústio for Dedalus Africa.

His translation of *By Night the Mountain Burns*, by Equatorial Guinean author Juan Tomás Ávila Laurel, was shortlisted for the 2015 Independent Foreign Fiction Prize.

SANDRA TAMELE

Sandra Tamele has a B.A in Architecture but her love for languages and reading inspired her to pursue a literary career instead. Since 2007, she has translated twenty-seven novels and short story collections written by, among others, Nobel Literature Laureates Wole Soyinka and Naguib Mahfouz.

Loose Ties, her translation of Yara Monteiro's novel, was longlisted for the Dublin Literary Award in 2023.

I

N'FŨCUA

Tchanaze woke with a scream. She'd dreamed of naked men dancing around her to funereal music, coarse hands fondling her beads and intimate parts. Her voice, usually so enchanting, now rang out tormented and shrill, freezing the blood of every man who heard it. Tchanaze, the fair maiden of Sena, fire and moon of the riverbanks, courted and coveted throughout the land, had become wife to the wickedest spirits of the underworld. Never again would her breasts herald bumper harvests or her waist channel the magic of the moon, for she'd contracted *n'fúcua*. Her thighs, where beads had once jingled in delightful whimsy, now ran red as her virginity poured unstoppably out of her.

All of this occurred in a time not so long ago on the banks of the Zambeze, the great river that leant the valley its name and spread mystery and misery wherever it flowed. How long it had done so was a matter of considerable debate, with some crossing hearts and swearing on the lives of the dead that the river was equal in age to the infinite number of sorghum and millet harvests it had witnessed, while others said it was as old as the hills and others still that it was older than the mountains, which, rugged and profane, sought to strangle the sacred watercourse somewhere between Sena and Dona Ana.

Sena was the village where Tchanaze was born, the moon forever full in her eyes, her skin aglow with all the colours of the firmament. Thus did she appear in visions to the seers of Kwamara, the sages of Caia and the witches of Kumalolo, who proclaimed that not for the next five hundred harvests would the valley be blessed with another so comely. The fair maiden was desired by every male from Sena to Nhángua, Caia to Kwamara, Kumalolo to Mutarara, Inhangoma and beyond, even as far as Gorongoza, and more: she was desired from the river sandbanks to the graveyard clay, for every male in the underworld loved her besides. Her parents, Suplera and Thomossene, had even been petitioned to hold a mass in her honour, under the lushest tree in Sena, to afford the village dead the chance to celebrate the girl's beauty too.

The locals were no strangers to remembering their dead for every year the Zambeze leapt from its banks and pulled a good number of villagers into its entrails. The drowned continued to worship Tchanaze from the underworld, and to damn Mbemba, for there was another fair maiden in Sena, one in whose eyes the moon never rose and whose beads made no sound. The tattoos on her chest were strange and menacing and the pertness of her breasts had never augured a bumper crop of sorghum like Tchanaze's had. Furthermore, from the very first moment the sun had shone on her newborn face, she'd suffered from a grave and incurable disease.

Thus Mbemba led a troubled life, forever cast in Tchanaze's shadow and the moon's most ominous shades. She lived on her own with her mother, Farença, for her father had been deported to the São Tomé plantations almost as soon as she'd been born. Farença had travelled high and low consulting witches, warlocks, healers and seers, anyone who might shed some light on the girl's affliction. These savants, whose forecasts could vary wildly when it came to predicting the Zambeze's rages, were unanimous in their diagnosis of Mbemba: she was a *mwali*, wife to the wickedest spirits in the valley. And so, reviled by every young buck in Sena, she was lusted after in the underworld, her body the scene of macabre orgies hosted by ghosts escaped from hell. She'd inherited a curse from her maternal great-grandmother, a woman who had, in life, appropriated the belongings of a dead person she had not known.

Because tradition dictated that a mother must guard her daughter's virginity until she'd found her a husband, Farença regularly monitored the *dhanda* cloth stuffed between Mbemba's legs. One day she found a sticky substance trickling down the girl's legs and looked up to find the *dhanda* soaked red. Knowing that no man from Mutarara to Derunde would go near a *mwali*'s thighs, Farença feared the worst. She took the girl to see a witch in Kumalolo and had her suspicions confirmed: *n'fúcua*. Having made Mbemba their woman, the evil spirits had now taken her virginity.

Kumalolo was a village to the south and east of Sena, perched on the banks of the Zambeze near Caia. It had a fierce reputation for witchcraft and for powerful witches who inhabited bodies that were not their own. These witches were the spirits of people who had died and been sent to hell, only to flee and take possession of another dead body. There were plenty of bodies to choose from for the river was thirsty in Kumalolo and quick to punish perceived slights and offences. Thus the witches of Kumalolo straddled the land of the living and the dead, allowing them to interpret the demands of the river spirits and instruct humans on how best to placate them. Little tended to be known about who the witches had been in life and so they were mysterious figures, as inscrutable as they were unscrupulous. Their appearances alone were enough to fill most people with dread for the corpses they adopted sported sinister tattoos and they wore beads with colours that were not of this world. In a sense they were apparitions, come to Kumalolo straight from the grave, but their presence was real enough and their temper and actions dictated everyone's fate.

Such a warlock had settled in Kumalolo shortly after the last sorghum harvest and quickly earned a reputation for being a grandmaster of the dark arts. People said he could establish a dialogue with any deceased relative, no matter how long dead, but also that he was mercurial and mischievous, even for a witch. No one knew where he'd come from or who his relatives were, so no one knew where he'd got his special powers from. But he went by the name of Mabureza and he'd taken possession of a body that was known, for it had belonged to one of three friends who drowned when their canoe capsized in the rapids. These three friends had been prominent figures and for a stranger to seize one of their corpses was considered brave or foolhardy.

Farença learned of Mabureza's reputation and promptly took Mbemba to see him. Kumalolo was more than a day's walk from Sena, and after navigating the Zambeze's numerous tributaries and confluents, they reached Mabureza's cabin sometime after dawn. The warlock appeared at the doorway to greet them and looked every inch the fugitive from hell. His body was covered in tattoos of the kind neither mother nor daughter had ever seen on a human before and he wore a necklace made of human fingers and teeth. He glowed not with moonlight or the sun's rays but with the satanic fires of all eternity.

He informed them of why they'd come as soon as he saw them: *n'fúcua*. This startled them but he went on to say that he knew the spirits who were feasting on Mbemba, knew them personally and by name, and that he could get them to leave; all Farença and Mbemba had to do was nominate another virgin maiden that the spirits could take as their wife instead.

'Tchanaze!' cried Mbemba almost hysterically. 'Tchanaze! Tchanaze! It has to be Tchanaze!'

'Okay! Okay!' Mabureza said before turning to Farença. 'Do you agree?'

Did she agree? Was her daughter's life not at stake? Of course she agreed, so she nodded, and Mabureza nodded too. Then he beckoned for Mbemba to enter the cabin and pointed for Farença to wait outside.

'Undress!' he said once he'd shut the door. Mbemba stripped down until she was naked aside from her *dhanda* and beads, conscious that their gleam was so lacklustre that no man from Sena to Caia to Cheringoma had ever noticed them. But now Mabureza stood staring at them. After a while he walked up to her and pulled them off, letting them spill to the floor and across the room. Then he removed her *dhanda* too and lifted her up. He held her in his arms for a while, then put her back down and contemplated her nudity for a few more minutes.

'Gather your things and put your clothes back on,' he said. 'My spirit friends will henceforth live inside Tchanaze. I'll prepare a potion for you to take back to Sena.'

She picked up her clothes while he fetched a pitcher of water and two calabashes. He filled the calabashes up halfway and then brought out a clay pot that looked like it had been stolen from somebody's grave. He took fragments of hair, teeth and bones out of the pot, which had undoubtedly been stolen from somebody's grave, dropped them into the calabashes and stirred. The water turned dark and viscous and began to look and smell like nothing Mbemba, or anyone else for that matter, had ever seen or smelled before. Then the warlock went over to the door and called Farença in.

'Take these calabashes to the *kuncito* where Tchanaze will be quarantined and spread the contents of one of them around her cabin. Do it at night, so as not to be seen, and do it naked, first your daughter and then you. Afterwards, dig a hole and bury the calabash, cover the hole and pee on it, both of you, understood?'

Farença nodded.

'Good, because what I have just said will surely come to

pass and there's more: the day Tchanaze dies, go back after she's been buried, strip naked again and dig up her body. Smear it with the contents of the other calabash, then rebury her along with that calabash. Fail to do any of this and the souls of the dead will rain great catastrophe down on you and your family for generations!' He handed Farença and Mbemba a calabash each. 'Pay heed for I have spoken!'

As soon as Tchanaze fell sick, Thomossene and Suplera took her to Kumalolo. They too had heard of Mabureza, but they'd also heard of another grandmaster witch who'd recently installed himself there. Beyond the reach of many, he was said to be even more powerful than Mabureza and so demonic he'd been given the name Phanga, after a killer dwarf who roamed the Gorongoza mountains. Like Mabureza, little was known of his origins but he too had taken possession of the body of one of three friends who'd drowned in the river when their boat capsized.

Tchanaze and her parents found Phanga standing bare-chested in the doorway of his cabin, eradiating the most satanic colours they'd ever seen.

'Do not come another step closer!' he cried when he saw them. 'Tchanaze, you have become the wife of my friends and companions in the underworld, tomb dwellers who flood this world with misfortune and despair. They found in you a beauty they'd never seen before and took you for their woman. Your body became theirs and will remain theirs until your death and beyond. I am Phanga and I have spoken!'

Tchanaze was too weak to understand but tears poured down her parents' faces.

'As for you, Thomossene,' the warlock thundered, 'you and your wife must build a cabin in the *kuncito* where your daughter will be placed in isolation. She must be left alone there, with no clothes, no food and no water, the spirits demand it, for they will feast on her until her demise. *Yhiààùuu*! I order this under penalty of death. *Yhiààùuu*! I am Phanga and I have spoken, *yhiààùuu*!'

There seemed to be no arguing with the warlock, a devil's disciple if ever they'd seen one, and so they hurried away, chastened but glad to be free of his presence. The birds in the trees cried out in sorrow as they made their way back to Sena, for Tchanaze's beauty was venerated by every living being in the valley. They walked through the night under the light of a moon they knew would never again illuminate the girl's belly. Indeed her body had already begun to emanate sinister colours, which through sobs, they sought to hide. But in vain.

'She's got *n'fúcua*!'

The cry went up as soon as the first villagers saw her and the refrain echoed from Sena to Mutarara, Murraça and as far away as Chupanga. Anything a witch ordered under penalty of death overrode all human laws and so a bamboo hut was erected in the furthest flung corner of the village and Tchanaze was placed in it without any clothes, food or drink. She lay naked but for the beads at her waist and breasts, which now glimmered only because of her tears. Lost souls and malignant ghosts would soon come to take their pleasure with her but they would bring her no sustenance and so she would die an inglorious death. She would scream into the night and she would die of *n'fúcua*, for this was the will of the spirits.

II

DEATH OF TCHANAZE

The night was so dark and dense that even the bats struggled to make out their prey. A stealthy wind hissed through the sedge grass and brought with it the sound of macabre music, redolent of the dead who roamed the village and so unnerved its inhabitants. Indeed it was generally thought that on nights as black as this one the dead came out seeking pleasure, wandering the village to visit lovers they'd had in life or to go down to the river to wash off the dust from their graves. They came out to satisfy their nostalgia for life, in other words, but also to meddle in the lives of the living, for fun or spite.

With the dead thus agitating, Tchanaze lay on the damp ground of a bamboo hut hidden beneath the branches of a large tree. Her breath was faint but enough to make her chest gently rise and fall. It was a pulse of fear and despair, and of shame too, at having had her maidenhood taken away by men long dead.

Her halting breath was not the only sound in the hut, indeed there was a fair riot of voices, indecipherable but enough to chill any living being to the bone. According to local lore, the spirits of N'tchimica, Nhambire and Tchinai, three friends who'd died together when their boat capsized, would have been at Tchanaze's side. All three had been witches in life, among the most feared men of their day, until their canoe had sunk in the river, bad weather striking just as they'd entered the rapid middle currents. They'd struggled harder than most, but like many before and after them, their efforts had proved no match for the fury of the waters. They'd been dragged down into the mud and clay by forces unknown and, as news spread of their passing, it was said that the Zambeze was as angry with mankind as it had ever been. And it was also said that any woman who died in Sena would be met by the three men on the other side, for they'd remained as firm friends in death as they'd been in life.

And so, as Tchanaze's body writhed around on the damp earth, N'tchimica, Nhambire and Tchinai's voices featured among the cacophony that reached her ears. She heard screams but saw no one. Invisible hands grabbed at her nakedness, loosened her *dhanda* and beads. A smell of roast meat teased her nostrils and there was even a crackle of firewood, but she could see no flames. When she tried to take a deep breath she found there was no air to gulp, so thick was the atmosphere with voices hovering over her in the dark. If she did not sense life slipping away from her, that was only because she was too overwhelmed by the spirits having their wicked way with her, spluttering out orgasms and drooling over her breasts, which they'd been denied the chance of ever seeing in life. Her own life, meanwhile, was a mere afterthought to the vagabond souls of Sena, Murraça and Caia desperate to get their fill, until it hung by a thread, held there only by the ancestors of one or two living acquaintances of the family and the unsatiated lust of three men who'd drowned together in a shipwreck.

The night grew gloomier still and a thin rain began to pepper the treetops. Then the wind became gustier and shook the canopy, sending heavier drops cascading down through the bamboo roof of the hut. A puddle formed around Tchanaze's body, allowing those ravaging her to quench their thirsts. She lay there all alone and yet surrounded by sex-starved ghosts and spirits bitter about having been sent to hell.

While Tchanaze lay prone inside the hut, Mbemba and Farença hid among the trees outside. They had taken good care not to be seen by anyone on the way but wanted to make sure there was no one keeping vigil. There was not, for a witch had ordered that a hut be built in the *kuncito* and that Tchanaze be left in it on her own. But Mbemba and Farença had their orders too.

They approached the hut and saw Tchanaze lying on the ground through the open door. She was convulsing, seemingly in her death throes, perhaps being enjoyed by invisible beings from the underworld. But the scene stirred neither mother nor daughter with mercy. On the contrary, hatred and vengeance swelled in their breasts, for Tchanaze's beauty had hypnotised every man in the region and her wiles had set hundreds of men's hearts aflame.

'Strip naked, my girl, and pour this liquid around inside the hut,' said Farença handing Mbemba one of the calabashes the warlock had given them. 'We must do as Mabureza said.'

While the girl whose beauty was celebrated with drumrolls writhed around in agony in the mud, the girl whose unattractiveness caused men to turn their backs took off her rain-soaked clothes. The rain ran down her naked bosom and onto her beads and tattoos, reminding her that hers was a body plagued by evil spirits. She snatched the calabash from her mother and rushed into the cabin, splashing the liquid liberally around the hut and with it the mortal remains of some poor soul who'd perished in the river's waters. She performed her task with relish, indifferent to Tchanaze's anguished cries and the gathering storm.

'That'll do,' said Farença, 'now it's my turn!' She stripped down and took the calabash from her daughter, who began to put her own clothes back on. Farença circled the outside of the hut administering the rest of the potion until every last drop had disappeared into the wet soil. If anything, Tchanaze's whimpering spurred her on for Farença, too, knew what it was to suffer. Her life had been a constant struggle since the day she'd given birth to a girl possessed by demons and she'd scoured the valley in a fruitless search for cures. But here was an opportunity to free Mbemba of her curse and Farença would not waver, for a mother's love knows no bounds. When the calabash was empty, she dug a hole in the soft earth with her hands and buried the vessel. Then she covered the hole to make sure nobody would find it and called Mbemba over so they could both urinate on the spot, just as Mabureza had instructed.

'Now we can go back to the village,' she said. 'May Tchanaze bring the spirits endless pleasure!'

They turned to go but were stopped in their tracks by a scream so loud and piercing it cut through the hammering rain and rang out into the night. It was a scream unlike anything they'd heard before and it sent shivers down their spines for it was unmistakeably the sound of a tortured soul pleading to be set free from the dungeons of hell. Where it had come from they could not say, but it had sent Tchanaze into spasms of further agony. Farença and Mbemba watched through the door as the pride and joy of Sena was dragged back and forth over the threshold between life and death.

'Come on,' said Farença taking her daughter's hand, for the scream had left Mbemba stricken. 'We've done what we came to do.'

In truth they were lucky the scream was all they heard and that the chorus of voices from beyond the grave eluded their ears. But as they crept away, the rain began to ease and the clamour died down. The spirits were departing having taken the life of the fairest maiden the valley had ever known. Tchanaze, apple of every young man's eye, lay lifeless in a pool of rainwater and ghostly fluids, her *dhanda* and beads floating by her side.

III

TCHANAZE'S BURIAL

Thomossene and Suplera counted four sunrises before going back to the cabin in the *kuncito* where they'd left their daughter to die in isolation. The laws the people of Sena lived by, passed down from generation to generation, advised four days grace and Campira, a local healer, confirmed it. He'd consulted the spirits of his ancestors who'd told him that Tchanaze would not live longer than four nights and that her body should be buried before five.

As parents of the deceased, Thomossene and Suplera led the funeral procession out to the cabin. They were followed by Campira, who would oversee the ceremony, and the entire village, for their daughter had been the love of everyone's life. Well not everyone's. In amongst the crowd of mourners was a certain mother and daughter. People tended to avoid looking the girl in the eye, for she was known to have *n'fúcua*, but if they'd looked that day they'd have seen she seemed strangely content and even radiant. Indeed Mbemba felt great. She still lacked Tchanaze's beauty and she knew Sena's young bucks were not about to start fighting over her just yet, but she felt at once cured and unburdened by the demise of the girl who'd always eclipsed her.

Thomossene and Suplera entered the hut and saw that their daughter was dead. They stepped forward and covered her body with a *capulana* as the crowd gasped in shock and grief. Tears welled up from the bottom of people's hearts, the girl having been the whole village's favourite daughter, and Mbemba and Farença cried too in an effort to disguise their glee.

Another *capulana* was placed beside the corpse ready to serve as a shroud but when Thomossene and Suplera went to roll their daughter onto it, they could not move her. Though soaked through with rain and the orgasmic fluids of beings from the afterlife, the corpse was rigid and stuck firm. Even Tchanaze's beads, which lay scattered all over the place, resisted being picked up.

'Wait!' said Campira. 'Let me handle this.'

The healer reached into his pouch, which he took with him everywhere, and removed a few bits of broken turtle shell. These fragments had been extracted from the depths of the Zambeze by his ancestors and passed down to him along with their meaning and magic. He tossed them on the ground a few times, read the messages they conveyed and told the crowd to build a bonfire. While everyone set about doing this, he took Thomossene and Suplera to one side.

'Your daughter is dead but she's pinned down by the spirits that inhabit her,' he said. 'Once the fire is lit, I will tell everyone to turn their backs and you will both urinate on the fire. These are my grandfather's instructions!'

The crowd soon got a good fire going and Campira told everyone to turn around, which they did, for the healer was a much-respected man. But Thomossene and Suplera struggled to fulfil their part of the bargain. A combination of stage fright and a lack of juice after so much crying meant that neither of them was able to pass so much as a drop of water. Furthermore, having to pee on a bonfire because malignant ghosts refused to leave your dead daughter's body was not just upsetting, it was a powerful reminder of the terrible hold the spirits had over their lives.

Sensing their predicament, Campira approached and handed them each a piece of a crocodile's toenail to chew on. A few seconds later they both felt their loins loosen and a pungent steam rose as their pee hissed into the flames.

'That'll do!' said Campira. 'Try moving her now.'

Thomossene and Suplera went back over to their daughter's body and pushed. She gave way easily this time and they were able to wrap her up in the *capulana* without any trouble. The crowd had turned back around to watch and were most impressed, but no one noticed the fragments of human hair, teeth and fingerbones that littered the ground. Campira, whose proficiency in the arts of black magic was beyond question in the eyes of the locals, failed to spot them too, and the spirit of his grandfather neglected to bring them to his attention.

The business of the corpse being impossible to shift was unexpected but Campira knew he had to press on. He summoned to his side the villagers he regularly called on for assistance, helpers who were not healers or witches themselves, but simply his ministrants. They followed orders and performed tasks that, in so much as they did not involve dealing directly with the spirits, did not require any special knowledge or powers. Campira told them to dig a hole beside the tree and this they gladly did, indeed some of them had even brought tools especially. They'd expected to do it because they knew as well as Campira that any man or woman who died in circumstances such as these had to be buried exactly where life drained out of them.

'Put the body in there!' Campira said to Tchanaze's parents, pointing to a box fashioned from bamboo and reeds. 'Then put the box in the hole!'

Thomossene and Suplera did as instructed, though less enthusiastically for they knew that their daughter would remain right there forever, distant from them and from the graves of the rest of the village dead.

The ceremony came to an end and the funeral procession made its way back into Sena. Farença and Mbemba tried to look suitably doleful though they felt only joy in their hearts. After all, Tchanaze's death brought them satisfaction not just because they'd rid themselves of *n'fúcua* but because they'd brought grief to those who deserved it.

That the corpse of the maiden who'd set hearts aflutter had refused to be moved became the talk of the village and the news soon spread to Mutarara and as far away as Cheringoma. Very few people who hadn't witnessed it couldn't believe it, for strange goings on governed by the fickle spirits of the underworld were a regular aspect of life in the valley. Everyone believed that the spirits of their ancestors roamed the land, that some wandered aimlessly and were harmless while others were wicked and fed the Zambeze's fury.

Tchanaze's unmovable corpse was undoubtedly worthy of comment, but something even more remarkable happened later on that night, for when darkness fell, Mbemba and Farença made their way back to the *kuncito*. Aside from the occasional mournful sob, the village was silent, the nightbirds withholding their song in respect for the solemnity of the day. The only light came from the flicker of fires glimpsed through cracks in cabin walls and so Mbemba and Farença walked guided only by their own evil intentions. Not a living soul saw them, the only witnesses to their passing being the phantasmagorical shadows of trees and the twinkling stars in the firmament. They carried the second calabash, containing a potion that was surely not of this world, and sought out the leafy tree under which Tchanaze had been buried.

'Right, let's undress and do as Mabureza instructed!' said Farença in a whisper. They stripped off, knelt down and started digging, feeling not the least sense of compunction about what they were doing. For a start, whenever she was naked, Mbemba was reminded that no young man had ever eyed up her breasts and beads and tattoos. She'd transferred her *n'fúcua* on to her rival and Tchanaze had died ravaged by evil spirits, for it would have been unfair to go through life with all the menfolk ogling just the one set off breasts and never her own.

They found Tchanaze's corpse just as they'd seen it laid to rest. It lifted easily out of the bamboo box and they peeled back the shroud of *capulanas* and smeared the potion all over her body. When the calabash was empty, they tucked it under the *capulanas*, wrapped the body back up and lowered it into the box. They put the box in the hole and filled it up again with soil. Then they got dressed and went back to the village.

They returned with their heads bowed to avoid being seen but also because, though they did not regret what they'd done, they knew it was considered deplorable. The villagers venerated the ground their dead ancestors lay in and the very notion of desecrating a grave was beyond the pale. Indeed it was so wicked that Mbemba, underneath her bowed head, couldn't help but smile.

IV

NEWS FROM INHANGOMA

At the start of the rainy season a woman who nobody knew settled in a remote part of Inhangoma, out in the reeds beyond the village of Mutarara. No one had ever seen her before and they'd never seen anyone like her either, for her face was the image of a full moon and her breasts and beads mesmerised any man who saw them. She was mysterious as well as beautiful, for she had no known friends or relatives and she lived on her own near the mangrove beside one of the Zambeze's lesser-known tributaries. She was no virgin maiden but the few Inhangoma men who had seen her spoke of her in rapturous tones and described her tattoos as markings inherited from the goddess of love.

Word of her charms spread up and down the river, crossed the bridge at Dona Ana and reached Sena. Her beauty was said to be of a kind that no living being had ever seen before, at least not in Inhangoma, for it was also said that she was the double of another celebrated beauty, one who had lived in Sena until not very long ago. Tchanaze's reputation, if not her face, was known in the villages of Inhangoma and witches there had started to proclaim that the new siren was a gift from the gods sent in compensation for the demise of the other.

Where the new beauty had come from nobody knew, when and why she'd settled in a remote part of Inhangoma remained a mystery and how she earned a living had yet to be ascertained. In other words, there were a lot of unanswered questions and they ate away at a certain healer from Sena. He decided to go and see for himself this woman whose beads had all the menfolk of Inhangoma smitten and the womenfolk envious.

Campira gathered what intelligence he could from the locals in Mutarara and struck out into the wilderness. The woman's hut proved easy to find, stood on its own as it was, and he knocked on the door just before sunset. There was no one home so he continued down to the riverbank, thinking she'd perhaps gone there to do her washing. Sure enough, he had not gone far when he saw her coming back the other way. She was carrying an earthenware pot on her head and water spilled from it over her body, making the beads around her neck glimmer in the sun.

When she reached him, he found he was unable to utter

a single word or even nod a greeting. She was of such divine grace that she could only have been a messenger sent by the gods to protect the good people of Inhangoma from the valley's evil spirits. Campira was utterly bewitched by her beauty but also by the fact that he'd seen her before, because he was staring at the very same woman who'd set hearts aflame in Sena. It was near impossible to comprehend, for he himself had administered her burial rites, but he was standing face to face with Tchanaze.

While Campira stood dumbstruck, she breezed past him, no doubt accustomed to men stopping to gawp at her, though his failure to pay her a compliment might have registered as odd. The healer took a deep breath, composed himself and followed.

He saw her enter her hut and hurried to catch up. She took the pot from her head and placed it in the corner of the room, relaxed and carefree. She clearly hadn't noticed him standing at the door.

'It cannot be you and yet it is,' he finally said. 'Tchanaze!'

She turned, bemused but smiling.

'As impossible as it sounds, it really is you, Tchanaze!' said Campira again. 'Or am I mistaken?'

'I don't know what you're talking about, sir,' she said calmly. 'My name is Fineja!'

'But that cannot be so! It is you, Tchanaze, I swear it on the lives of the dead of the last flood!'

'No, you're mistaken. Leave me alone, please.'

'Then tell me, what are you doing here? Where did you come from? Who are your parents?' said the healer. 'I mean, you're dead, Tchanaze, I officiated at your funeral! How do you explain that?'

She looked nervously at him but gave no answer. Then she suddenly rushed passed him, out the door and into the reeds. She let out a scream as she went and it sent shivers down Campira's spine, for it was unlike any scream he'd heard before. Fear overtook him and he set off running too, not after her but back the way he'd come. He was sure he'd just seen Tchanaze, the fair maiden of Sena, but that scream had belonged to someone else, or indeed something else. It was the scream of an evil spirit, the kind that lived inside women and made them their wives.

All the same, he was convinced that the woman was Thomossene and Suplera's daughter. He knew he could not go back to Sena with news like that unless he was absolutely sure, so he decided to stay in Mutarara for the night and visit the girl again the next morning. He'd probe her and demand some answers this time. If she was not Tchanaze then why did she look so very like her? And if she was Tchanaze, well, never mind what was she doing in Inhangoma, what was she doing alive?

But when he went back the next day, not only was she not there but the hut itself was gone. After puzzling over this for a while, he walked into the reeds and found the path to the river where he'd seen her the previous day. He followed it back and forth but still couldn't find the hut. He retraced his steps back towards Mutarara and started all over again. But still he found nothing, nothing but the smell of mildew that blew in off the river and the occasional bird that swooped over his head. There was no sign of a hut or a woman who claimed she was called Fineja.

After searching fruitlessly for another few hours, his eyes began to tire and the whole area became tinged in a strange glow. He was at a loss to explain what could have happened to either the woman or the hut and so he decided to do what he always did when he felt powerless in the face of impossible questions: consult his ancestors.

He walked back through the reeds and crouched down where he thought the hut had been. Then he closed his eyes and turned towards the setting sun, silently evoking the spirits of his ancestors and all who had drowned in the great river's turbulent waters. There he remained, in the grip of supernatural forces and distant from the world around him, until a new day dawned.

As the sun rose behind him, the sound of a creaking door brought him back to reality. He opened his eyes and saw a hut just a few metres away from where he was squatted. He stood up and walked towards it, confirming that it was indeed the hut he'd been searching for the previous day. There was a woman standing in the doorway holding a calabash in her hands. She looked beautiful, certainly the most beautiful creature the region of Inhangoma had ever known.

'Tchanaze, I'm Campira,' he said and he walked purposefully towards her. 'I'm here because I know who you really are!'

'No, you're mistaken,' she replied uncomfortably, 'that is not my name!'

'I know it's you, Tchanaze! What are you doing here?'

As he spoke, he reached out a hand and touched her on the arm. She recoiled and screamed, and he took a step back. It was the same scream he'd heard before, it had come out of the mouth of this woman and from the depths of hell. Then she rushed past him and ran off into the reeds again. He turned to give chase but knew it was impossible. He stood there feeling helpless, though he had established what he'd come back for. He was now certain that the great beauty of Inhangoma was none other than the fair maiden of Sena.

V

SUPLERA AND THOMOSSENE GET A SHOCK

As was only to be expected, the news Campira brought back from Inhangoma came as a great shock to the dead girl's parents. They refused to believe him at first, despite him swearing on the graves of all his ancestors and on the lives of everyone who'd drowned in the last flood. Besides, he couldn't be mistaken, for he'd witnessed the girl being born and had watched her grow, he'd even administered her funeral rites. He urged them to go to Kumalolo immediately and consult a witch there, one whose capabilities he could personally vouch for, and seek a second opinion on a phenomena that was highly unusual, but not necessarily unprecedented. Campira vaguely recalled his dearly departed grandfather, from whom he'd inherited the healing art, talk of a similar case in Chupanga. And Campira said more besides: he reminded the couple that the souls of the dead in the valley were capable of many things and some of these things were only understood by satanist warlocks, such as the man he was recommending they visit in Kumalolo.

He realised that what he'd just said had frightened Thomossene and Suplera, for they shook with a cold that wasn't there, a cold known only to men whose canoe had capsized in the Muananhoca straits. He felt anxious too, not just because the case was so similar to the one his grandfather had mentioned, but because he'd overseen the girl's burial and worried he'd perhaps failed in his duty if the girl were still alive. He volunteered to go with them to Kumalolo and he said they would leave that very night and in secret, so that no one else in the village might know about it. Speaking quietly and solemnly, so as not to disturb the dead, he told them they must prepare for the trip right away and he asked them to bring him a black hen.

It was the middle of the afternoon and the sky was clear but with dark clouds moving towards the setting sun, a sure sign that the weather would turn before the day was done. The recently deceased began to lick their lips in anticipation of the rains that would soon quench their thirst and sure enough, by the time Suplera came back with a hen, the first drops started to fall.

The hen had once been Tchanaze's favourite but now

Campira slit its throat using nothing but his own teeth. His eyes nearly popped out of their sockets as he bit into it, frightening Thomossene and Suplera all the more and reminding them that, although Campira was a friend and a neighbour, he was also one of very few men in the valley who understood the mysteries of the land, the great river they slept beside and the souls who lived in its sandbanks. The healer drank the blood that spurted from the chicken's neck and then passed it to the couple to drink from too. Then he told Thomossene to dig a hole at the back of the house. When this was done he poured the rest of the chicken's blood into it and buried the carcass. Then he turned to the couple and told them to go inside and wait.

Once he was alone, Campira knelt down on the pile of sand that covered the dead hen and began to evoke his ancestors. He wanted to send a message to his grandfather to make sure their trip to Kumalolo was a success. He prayed silently at first but then with howls that pierced the walls of Thomossene and Suplera's home and reached every house in the village. It was a sound that commanded the respect of everyone for they knew they were the howls of a man communicating with his ancestors on the other side. Campira stood up, still in prayer, and urinated on the mound, then waited in silence.

'You, man, go and urinate!' he said upon returning to the cabin. 'And you, woman, get ready, you're next!'

Thomossene and Suplera did as they were told. They knew that when Campira spoke like this he was to be obeyed, for he was conveying the will of the spirits.

'Yhiàààuu, yhiàààuu! Follow me to Kumalolo!' Campira wailed, and off he went, leaving Thomossene and Suplera unsure whether they were still in the presence of their neighbour or if some demonic being had taken possession of him. 'Follow me!'

They followed. The sky by now gleamed with lightning strikes and drops of rain, which fell softly at first but soon grew in strength until large puddles formed. Curious shadows appeared to dance with joy on hut walls, until the glow of lamps became lost in the downpour. The incessant rumbles and flashes suggested the sky would deliver its refreshment until dawn, but the couple followed the healer into the night, of course they did, because Tchanaze could not possibly be alive, they knew better than anyone else that their daughter was dead.

They walked through the night, passing the villages of Caia and Tchangadeia, crossing rivers and streams under an intense downpour. The rain left them cold to the bone and their teeth chattered, until finally morning broke and the dawn of a new day brought respite. They reached Kumalolo with the rain fizzling out and they made straight for the Zambeze riverbank, where the witch's hut stood in the thick reeds. He opened the door before they'd had a chance to knock, for he'd seen them coming in a dream and had immediately woken from it. Besides, he'd already been told by his people to expect them and he'd spoken to Tchinai in his sleep. Tchinai was one of three inseparable friends who'd been swallowed by the Zambeze when their canoe capsized and it was in his flesh and bones that the warlock now lived. He stood there and stared at them and Thomossene and Suplera saw that it was the same witch they'd visited before, the one who went by the name of Phanga. Indeed there could be no mistaking him: he was more skeleton than man and his tattoos and facial features suggested none other than the devil himself.

'Campira,' Phanga said before they'd spoken to him, 'take Thomossene and his wife back to Sena and carry on to Mutarara and Inhangoma. They must make contact with that woman at once. Then bring them back to me. And hear this: I will be waiting for you, but hurry!'

He shut the door after he'd said this, for he had his rituals to perform. Mornings were when he communed with his people, the dead and the damned, for Phanga was believed to have escaped from the fires of hell.

Screams soon began to emerge from the hut, the likes of which Thomossene and Suplera had never heard. It was not the screaming of a madman or the wailing of a drunkard heading home after too much *nipa*, nor was it the whooping of a reveller taken by the beat of a drum on a starry night. No, it was a screaming so deafening it could only have come from another world, and then the screams became yells, cries of rage, damnations hurled from every corner. This was what it took for Phanga to reach his people from the skeleton he now inhabited in Kumalolo, and to reach Tchinai, the former owner of that skeleton. Campira, too, began sweating all over, a hot sweat that contrasted with the coolness of the early morning. It wasn't out of fear but something he couldn't quite explain, something deep inside him that told him this was a man from another world who'd come to Kumalolo to practise black magic with unrestrained abandon.

Thomossene and Suplera had a similar feeling and they began to shake with fear, a fear that only grew as the infernal being began to launch himself against the walls of his hut.

No wonder Phanga's fame had spread so quickly through the valley. He was recommended by everyone from Inhangoma to Mutarara to Sena, and even as far away as Cherongoma and Muanza. Anyone anywhere who wanted their neighbour dead, or their brother or sister dead, or even their father dead, went to see Phanga for he would satisfy their request without so much as pausing for thought. If a man wanted to kill his best friend and make off with his wife, he turned to this master witch and cold-blooded sorcerer. People started calling him Phanga and his fame grew until he became the most coveted warlock in Kumalolo, his extravagant services sought from as far away as Save, Sussundenga and Alto-Molócue.

'Let's go back to Sena!' said Campira, turning towards Thomossene and Suplera. 'We must do exactly as the warlock said.'

Thomossene and Suplera knew very well that they must do exactly as the warlock said, not least because they could tell that even Campira, the most admired witch in Sena, was in awe of the man's powers.

VI

IN INHANGOMA

Thomossene, Suplera and Campira reached Sena before the sun had risen over the horizon and with one or two stars still twinkling in the sky. But sticking to Phanga's instructions, they carried on straight to Inhangoma, crossing the bridge at Dona Ana and pausing only to contemplate the murky waters of the Zambeze. The lost souls of those who'd died building the bridge were said to reside there, for the mountain spirits had demanded a good many lives be sacrificed in compensation for such an abuse of the landscape.

They'd been walking for hours and the grimaces on

Thomossene and Suplera's faces had become engrained. They thought about *n'fúcua* and the hold it had over their lives, for they'd had to worry about it since the day Tchanaze was born. Every parent worried about their child contracting *n'fúcua*, but everyone knew the evil spirits favoured beautiful girls and Thomossene and Suplera had begotten the most beautiful of them all. But she'd grown up healthy and strong and she'd been just about to enter womanhood, when *n'fucua* had finally struck. They'd had to forsake her, isolate her in the *kuncito* and abandon her to the lust of demons and certain death. And yet even now, with their daughter buried in the ground, *n'fúcua* continued to haunt them by flaunting the idea that Tchanaze might be alive after all.

Dark clouds hung ominously over the mountains as the trio skirted around Mutarara and set off into the Inhangoma wilderness. Campira led them through the reeds and eventually to a pile of granite rocks. Thomossene and Suplera could tell that the rocks bothered the healer and they came to realise that this was the spot where the cabin was supposed to be. There was nothing to suggest a house had ever stood there, no trace of human activity and no sign of a woman who went by the name of Fineja.

Campira was indeed exasperated. Had he got confused and brought them to the wrong place? No! He would have sworn on the lives of his dead ancestors that this was the very spot. Right where the rocks were now piled high there had once been a hut and in it had lived a woman who had once been dead.

'Let's go back to the village,' he said. 'I need to consult my people about this.'

Thomossene and Suplera persuaded him to look around first and make sure he hadn't lost his bearings. He conceded, though their lack of faith rankled, and they spread out into the reeds and searched for the cabin. They heard hippos and crocodiles in the riverbanks but they found no woman and no dwelling. Exhausted, they made their way back to Mutarara ready to bed down for the night and resume their search the next day.

The next day dawned calm and serene and the sun was high up over the horizon by the time they'd returned to the mangroves. A fresh smell of sedge blew in from the other side of the Zambeze while on their bank sorghum and millet swayed in the wind. Campira got ready to commune with his people but again Thomossene suggested they have a scout around first. The healer again acquiesced, chastened that they doubted him, but after searching through the reeds and the sorghum and millet, all they found was the same pile of rocks. Campira inspected them and saw that they'd come from the deepest depths of the riverbed.

They were interrupted in their activities by someone returning from the river. It was a woman but not Fineja. She was bare-chested and water ran down from her wet hair over her body and breasts, which looked unlikely to ever herald bumper harvests, and her tattoos and beads were similarly plain. They asked her if she knew the whereabouts of a woman who'd recently settled in the area. She said she'd heard that someone lived in a hut nearby and pointed into the brambles. She claimed to be very busy, otherwise she'd have shown them the way, but said it was easy to find. She rushed off and Thomossene and Suplera followed Campira into the scrub.

They soon came upon another pile of rocks. These looked just like the other ones to Thomossene and Suplera, but Campira pointed out that they had an inner glow. This suggested they'd come not from the depths of the river but somewhere much deeper: the dungeons of hell.

They returned to Mutarara with the couple feeling unsettled and demoralised. Campira tried to placate them and sent Thomossene off to get a red cloth from a nearby cantina. He said he'd need it to make an incantation because if they were ever going to locate the woman, their daughter, the beauty of Inhangoma and former fair maiden of Sena, he would have to make contact with his late grandfather.

Thomossene returned with the cloth and Campira told them to wait in the village while he went back down to the river. He set off immediately, walking at a brisk pace. The wind that had started the day as a gentle breeze was now furiously bending the trees, but this was only to be expected in Inhangoma at that time of year, as was the prospect of rain. The healer tried to push such thoughts out of his mind and focus on the mystic phenomena in hand.

When he got to the first pile of river rocks, he plunged into the reeds, heading in the opposite direction to the infernal rocks. He took off his vestments and changed into the cloth, which was of a purplish red colour with dark patches. He took up a crouching position and proceeded to yell in a language that no one on earth other than he spoke or understood. The wind grew stronger and threatened to become a storm, but he continued with his chant until he'd made contact with his grandfather. A storm did then materialise and heavy rain and even hailstones bounced off his back. But he remained right where he was, hunkered down amongst the prickly reeds, untroubled by the rain or the crocodiles and hippos that lurked in the riverbanks. Though it seemed otherwise, he was in a deep sleep in which strange things were revealed to him, things only he had witnessed, alongside assurances that he would be helped in solving this mystery and future ones besides.

With the coming of dawn, the storm passed and Campira awoke from his trance, unscathed by hail or hippo. He took off his cloth and changed back into his regular clothes. He was a new man and his face beamed with a triumphant smile, for his grandfather had spoken to him and given him precise instructions on what do. He went back to the village and greeted his companions like a champion returned.

'Let's go and find Tchanaze!' he said. 'Come on, Thomossene! Get your wife and follow me!'

Thomossene and Suplera looked at the healer, so happily soaked to the bone, and exchanged puzzled looks. But they got up and followed him back into the wilderness, back to where they'd found the pile of rocks from hell. Only now, instead of a pile of rocks, there was a hut.

It was a hut like any other in the area, with bamboo walls and a dry grass roof, but it had definitely not been there the previous day. Thomossene and Suplera began to feel uneasy because the sudden appearance of a hut meant black magic and the impenetrable actions of river spirits, but then they heard a familiar melody and felt instant comfort and joy. It was a melody their daughter had often sung when she was alive, indeed she'd sung it with the same cadence and tenderness they were hearing now.

'Tchanaze, come out!' Campira said in a voice that startled

them with its authority. 'Come on out!'

The melody stopped and the ensuing silence weighed heavily, alleviated only by a distant burst of birdsong. Then the door of the cabin opened and there she was, their daughter, looking divine.

They blinked and rubbed their eyes but it was her alright, the woman who'd brought spark and flame to every man's heart. Her beads and tattoos were unmistakable, her breasts undoubtedly those that had augured good harvests. It was Tchanaze alright, the fair maiden of Sena, venerated by spirits past, present and future. Thomossene and Suplera were so awestruck they took a step back.

'I am not Tchanaze,' the woman shrieked, her voice satanic, her breath icy. 'I am not Tchanaze!'

Then she rushed out of the hut and charged past them into the bush.

VII

BACK TO KUMALOLO

Phanga had told them to go back to Kumalolo after they'd been to Inhangoma but they all agreed they needed to stop off in Sena and get some rest. They would leave for Kumalolo at nightfall the following day.

Thomossene and Suplera needed to not only rest but gather their thoughts. They'd just met someone who appeared to be their daughter, but their daughter was dead. The entire village, themselves included, had taken part in her burial. They therefore struggled to believe what they'd seen with their own eyes and they were reluctant to go back to Kumalolo again.

Tragedy had come knocking at their door, but they'd made their peace with it. Why go through all this fresh torment when they knew better than anyone that their daughter was gone?

Nevertheless, they could not easily shake a new nagging doubt: if the woman in Inhangoma was not Tchanaze, then who was she? The only way to answer that question was to go and consult Phanga again. Having opened themselves up to the mystery, they had no choice but to follow it through to its conclusion. Because if their daughter was gone then who was the hermit in the reeds who looked just like her? They were only sorry they hadn't spoken to her.

The sun disappeared over the horizon and night brought a smattering of stars and a humid breeze. They reached Kumalolo as dawn broke and went straight to the warlock's cabin. Everything was silent aside from the whisper of the river running through the valley, the steam of its breath serving as a reminder that in its depths lived the drowned of all eternity. They found Phanga sitting at the door to his hut, his eyes fixed on some invisible point on the horizon. As with their previous visit, he'd been expecting them, having dreamed of their coming. He stood up and yelled: 'Do not come any closer! Stay right where you are!'

The three visitors came to an immediate halt a few metres from the hut. Phanga's silhouette filled the doorway, radiating the wickedest colours of the underworld.

'I can tell from your faces that you saw her but you did not speak to her!' he growled. 'Wait out here until I call for you!'

He disappeared into his cabin, his beads jangling on his skeletal frame, and closed the door. They soon heard him howling and prowling around the room. They sat down ready to wait while he ran through his highly involved morning routine, but in fact it wasn't long before he summoned them in.

They found him wearing a mask made of different animal pelts, quite unlike anything any of them had ever seen before, and in his right hand he brandished an item that looked like a short-handle broom but with bristles made from straw and human hair. He waved it around manically and began to scream, a truly demonic shriek that recalled the sound wild cats made when they showed up on the outskirts of Sena. He paused from his wailings to slam the door and unceremoniously hurl a buffalo-skin at them. They sat down on the skin and watched him throw himself on the floor and start thrashing around. He appeared to be trying to shake himself free of something. Then he went silent and still.

After a while he got up and sat down on a stool made from black wood and covered in a red cloth. He stared them up and down, slowly but almost timidly. Then his tattooed mouth opened and out came a greeting: 'Hello.'

This was not something that had happened before, indeed the man seemed incapable of common courtesies. But it was not the greeting itself that surprised them. The word had come out of the warlock's lips but not with his voice, rather it was the soft and halting voice of a woman.

Thomossene and Suplera froze in terror, though Campira, well-versed in the customs of witchcraft, remained relatively unfazed.

'Do you know who it is that greets you?' asked the female voice, which sounded old, somewhat tired. 'Do you know who I am? I don't think so, let me explain. I am the deceased Nhantete. I have been dead for many floods now, stuck in the

Zambeze's sand and clay banks. In life, I took possession of a dead person's belongings, someone who was a stranger to all but who lived in the land of Sena. As a consequence of my actions, I contracted a sickness deemed to be incurable, a sickness named *n'fúcua*, which tormented me until my death. Do you hear me?'

They nodded, though none of them dared speak, not even Campira.

'I am here talking to you now because the man whose body I am in asked me to and because I think you deserve to know the truth about Tchanaze. So hear this: go home, gather drums and dig up your daughter's grave. Disinter the corpse and take it to a witch named N'tchira who lives in the Gorongoza mountains. But first follow the instructions of my good friend Phanga. I have spoken!'

The woman stopped talking and there was an uncomfortable silence, finally broken by a deep, piercing cry that would have sent shudders through even the bravest man alive. Phanga seemed to have returned. He threw himself, or the skeleton he inhabited, on the floor and thrashed around in great contortions as if sharp pains were attacking his entire body. The three visitors watched in appalled amazement as he rolled from one side of the hut to the other. The warlock was disturbingly strange and clearly possessed by demon spirits. He was the most frightening witch they'd ever met and they wondered if he might even be the leader of every malignant soul in the Zambeze basin. But the worst was still to come. He stood up and started banging his head against the wall, then slammed his whole body against it, repeatedly, letting out cries and wails of the kind usually heard only on the darkest of nights when the dead went out to play. Trails of blood began to run from his mouth, a mouth that could emit other people's voices and issue orders from people long dead. Orders like dig up your daughter, orders that had to be obeyed to avoid the wrath of the spirits.

The hut fell silent again. The warlock lay prone on the damp floor, as inert as a corpse, though they could see that he was still breathing and blood flowed from his mouth. Thomossene, Suplera and Campira looked on dumbly, unsure of what to do, hoping he'd stir sooner or later. They all knew that the gruesome scene they'd just witnessed was part of the ritual that enabled witches to speak to the dead but only Campira understood that the longer a person had been dead, the harder they were to reach and the more onerous was the ritual.

All the same, what happened next took them all by surprise. The warlock sprang to his feet and sat back down before his guests as if nothing had happened. His body had just been subjected to a terrible pummelling, but aside from a few coagulating dribbles of blood, he showed no sign of injury or pain.

'As you've heard I will now instruct you on what to do next,' he said, panting a little but speaking in a voice that was for the most part clear and sharp, and male. 'Campira, go and wait outside!'

The healer stood up without hesitation and left the hut.

'My friends,' said Phanga, looking first to Thomossene and then to Suplera, 'you must exhume Tchanaze and take what you disinter to N'tchira in Gorongoza, do you hear me?'

'Yes, we hear you,' said Thomossene. 'The lady who just

spoke to us said the same thing.'

'Good, then you know what to do. But let me warn you, N'tchira is almost impossible to reach. I, for one, do not know of anyone alive who has seen him!'

The great witch looked at the couple out of the corner of his eye and saw them exchange nervous glances.

'We are prepared to try if it will bring our daughter back, sir!' said Thomossene, his voice barely recognisable as his own, so cut through with fright was it. But it was true that he would do anything to recover their daughter and bring joy back into their lives.

'Excellent, excellent!' said the warlock. 'But listen carefully to what I am about to say: once you have committed to it, there's no going back, under penalty of death for you and disaster for your entire generation! Understood?'

'Yes, sir!' Thomossene and Suplera said in unison.

'Very well, if that is your wish then so will it be done!' Phanga said. Then he stood up and went over to some baskets standing by the window. He opened one and took out a knife and a flask containing a potion. It was a purple liquid and when he took off the lid a pungent smell filled the room reminiscent of a washed-up boat in the aftermath of a flood.

'Lie face down!'

It was clearly an order and they both did as they were told. Phanga bent over their backs with the knife and proceeded to make a series of tiny cuts in their skin. Inoculations, the locals would have called them, but each incision brought a jolt of pain. It was a strange pain too, for it rushed through them from stomach to intestines to kidneys and on to other body parts they didn't know they had.

'Be brave, my children, be brave!' Phanga said as he made more cuts and blood started to dribble from their bodies into the damp earth of the floor. Then he poured the purple potion from the flask onto their backs and smeared it into their wounds. The pain disappeared as if by magic. The couple knew they'd just had a concoction from hell rubbed into their skins but they also knew it had stopped the pain they'd been feeling instantly, or something resembling pain.

'Now get up and go!' Phanga said, his voice loud and gruff. He opened the door for them. 'Go on, get out!'

They picked themselves off the floor and hastened to the door.

'And don't forget to do everything Campira tells you!' Phanga yelled, globules of blood and spittle flying from his mouth. 'I am Phanga and I have spoken!'

Campira saw that Phanga's mood was changing fast. It would soon be time for the warlock to commune with his kin and they did not want to get in the way of that. 'Come on,' the healer urged, 'quickly!.

VIII

TCHANAZE DISINTERRED

They walked back to Sena knowing that they would have to disinter Tchanaze: a witch had ordered it and a witch's instructions had to be carried out. Witches expressed the will of the spirits and the spirits ensured that traditions established by people long dead were upheld, which was what allowed different generations to coexist in relative harmony.

Thomossene and Suplera would have to rely on Campira once again for guidance. It was their fate to be the parents of Tchanaze, the fairest maiden and wearer of the brightest beads, who had died of *n'fúcua* and was now to be dug up. The healer would preside over what would be an unprecedented ceremony, never seen before in Sena or anywhere else in the valley. Word soon spread to the villages of Mutarara and Murraça and through the lands of Marromeu, Cheringoma, Muanza and beyond, and people came, out of curiosity, reverence and awe.

Campira was as perplexed by the instruction as anyone else. Phanga had surpassed his expectations, which wasn't to say Campira was intimidated by what he had to do, just that he knew it was the devil's business. What the elders had always said was now being confirmed to him: the Zambeze was a refuge for fugitives from hell.

He knew his reputation as a healer hung on the success of the exhumation and he accepted this and got on with organising the macabre occasion. He ordered pitchers and pitchers of alcohol, made from millet, to be left out for the spirits to drink, and he summoned every ceremonial dance group in the region, to ensure that the beat never let up. Given the complex and solemn nature of the act, he would need as many ministrants at his disposal as possible, so he assembled all his disciples and every savant around, anyone with any experience whatsoever of practising witchcraft, even mere apprentices, and with them he formed a council. They would all need to wear red *capulanas*, so he dispatched someone to procure them. He then sent for a dozen black spotted hens, which they would sacrifice over Tchanaze's grave, and he announced that prayers would commence before dawn the following Sunday.

The Sunday came amidst a fervour of great expectation, but it began like any other day, the sun's glow peeping over the horizon to the east. The disinterment cortège left the village and made its way slowly out to the *kuncito.* Campira took the lead, dressed in a black *capulana*, with his ministrants behind him, dressed in red, followed by the parents of the girl who was about to be dug up. The rest of the village and visitors fell in behind, Mbemba and Farença among them, with those at the front carrying the pitchers and hens. The drummers brought up the rear, though the funereal songs they chanted to begin with were so solemn they required only the occasional rasp of a tambourine. There was a general sense of trepidation concerning what they were about to do, though they all knew that whatever came out of a witch's mouth had to be obeyed. There was no going back once a witch had been consulted, not unless you wished to incur the fury of spirits from hell.

The procession reached the edge of the village and the start of the bush. Campira led them over to a large tree under which a pile of sand had been laid to indicate where the grave was. Those carrying pitchers were told to put them down by the sand and Campira made the crowd form a circle. He asked for quiet and the drummers fell silent, though some sobbing could still be heard, as well as the clucking of hens. These the healer now called for. One by one, he broke their necks with his teeth and handed them back to a ministrant for them to aim the spouting blood on Tchanaze's grave. When all the hens had thus been sacrificed the ministrants threw the carcasses on the now-scarlet sand and knelt down. In a high-pitched, piercing voice, Campira proceeded to evoke the Sena dead and say things to them in words few people present could decipher. By the time he'd finished, the sun's rays had begun to force their way down through the canopy of the trees. The first part of the ceremony was over, it was time for the disinterment.

Campira got to his feet and told his disciples to start digging. The crowd gulped as hoes were thrust into the ground and there was another round of sobbing. But the ministrants stuck firmly to their tasks. They knew that if the procedure was a success it would reflect well on them and bring them a degree of fame, maybe even set them up for a promising career. So they dug hard and they persevered for several hours, until it became clear to everyone that their efforts were in vain. No matter how much they dug, the hole never got any bigger, indeed it seemed to refill itself. What they were trying to do evidently went against the will of the spirits and it was unwise to challenge the combined strength of the ghosts of all eternity.

Astonishment and fear spread through the crowd as people realised what was happening. Even the master of ceremonies was at a loss to explain it. Had he made a mistake? Had he forgotten a key stage in the ritual? Whatever it was, the healer was shaken. His wisdom and standing, along with the prestige of all his men, was being publicly challenged. He fell to his knees, arched his back and threw his arms up to the skies.

'Tchassassa, my dear grandfather, and everyone else in the Nhalúguè clan,' he cried, 'aid me in my work, which is after all your work too. N'tchimica, Nhambire, Tchinai, everyone who died in the last flood, and the flood before that, I beg you, have mercy on me in front of this crowd. Help me, please, your humble servant, Campira.'

He lowered his arms and reached for his pouch. He took out a good pinch of snuff and spread it into the earth around the tree. He evoked the spirits while he did this, the dead ancestors of everyone present and all the ghosts of everyone who'd ever perished in the great river, no matter how long ago. When he'd finished he stood up and spoke in a voice that was at once serious and serene: 'Start digging again!'

This the ministrants did and the crowd looked on with a mixture of fascination and horror. The afternoon sun warmed their heads but what they were witnessing chilled their bones. Dark forces were at play, the lost souls that everyone feared were themselves manifesting.

But this time the ministrants quickly came upon what they were looking for. Campira leaned over them and saw the box made of bamboo and reeds. The spirits had answered his prayers.

He stood back to let his helpers lift the box out. Much to the surprise of anyone who'd seen it buried, it hadn't changed a bit since that day, several months ago. But a much greater surprise was soon to come. When the healer took off the lid and looked into the box, he saw not the body of a girl but a cat. It had been wrapped in *capulanas*, just as Tchanaze had been, but appeared to have been dead for a few hours at the most.

The crowd gasped but Campira kept his poise. He told Suplera to pick the dead cat up and cradle it in her arms. Phanga had told them to dig up Tchanaze and take whatever they found to Gorongoza, he hadn't said it would necessarily be their daughter's body. He hadn't said it would be a dead cat either, or any other kind of dead animal for that matter, which was a little strange. But the point was he hadn't told them what to expect, he'd merely told them to take what they disinterred to N'tchira, the great witch of Gorongoza. And that was what they would do, for this was the devil's work and it would be foolish to defy the warlock in such matters.

All of that said, when the cortège headed back into the

village, with Thomossene and Suplera at its head, Campira stayed on behind. He crouched down by the tree and prepared to once again evoke the spirits of people who were long since dead but forever implicated in the life of the valley. The crowd had left confused and silent, holding back the pain they felt in their breasts and muttering about the terrible power those who dwelled in the murky depths of the river had over them. There was some drumming and chanting but not much and all sight and sound of the procession was soon lost to the healer. The healer's silhouette was likewise soon lost to the dark, for the kind of ceremony he'd just presided over ate up a lot of daylight.

Later that night, Campira knocked on Thomossene and Suplera's door. There was no one else around and no nightbirds could be heard. When he went inside he found Suplera sitting on a mat by the fireplace with the dead cat in her arms, tears streaming down her face. Her eyes burned red in the glare of the flames and the crackle of the fire muffled her sobbing. The healer greeted the couple with a blank expression. Indeed he'd walked in like a living corpse, his face a stranger to itself, his body weak and limp. There were no pleasantries, no displays of warmth or consolation, he simply shut the door behind him and sat down.

'My friends, I am sorry about what you are having to go through but you must be patient and brave. Your daughter will return,' he said. 'According to my consultations, you must leave for Gorongoza at dawn. Once there, upon entering the mountains but before coming upon a settlement, ask for N'tchira.'

The healer looked at them as if to invite questions. They

hadn't any.

'Safe travels,' he said. 'I'll be waiting for you when you get back.'

IX

THE JOURNEY TO GORONGOZA

Cockerels cried and dogs howled, stirring up nostalgic memories for those who had, in life, jumped out of bed at such sounds and headed for the river to lay traps and cast bait. The Zambeze's waters could, by turns, be wild and still but it was home to a great abundance of fish. In the villages that dotted the banks on both sides, fish was the staple of every household diet and the favourite dish of many. A particularly large variety of fish was to be found in the Muananhoca straits where an islet would appear at the height of the dry season. It was said, indeed people swore on it, that the secret to this glut of fish, and especially the prevalence of beard-fish, much appreciated by locals, lay in the fact that thousands of lives had been lost there. Every year the river lured fishermen out into its currents and pushed them into the straits where they capsized and drowned, bringing grief to the living but nourishment to the waters.

The cockerel's cry was also the signal for Thomossene and Suplera to get up and embark on their journey. Get up but not wake up, for the spirits of their ancestors had failed to comfort them sufficiently and neither of them had slept a wink. But the rest of the village was still fast asleep as they left their hut, Suplera clutching the dead cat to her chest. Their destination was Gorongoza and a witch named N'tchira, after a magic wand made from animal pelts. Campira had told them it would take at least a week to reach Gorongoza, for they had first to cross the plains beyond Sena and then navigate the forest that led into the mountain foothills.

And so it proved. After several days spent out in the open, lighting campfires at night to keep warm and ward off wild animals, they got their first glimpse of the forest. They knew they had to pass through it to reach the mountains beyond and a peak that was a source of eternal mystery. The range was so immense that the human eye could not take it in and it was impossible to comprehend its true contours. The highest point was an optical illusion even to those who lived nearby, for people did live in Gorongoza, in the foothills and forests, alongside wild animals and in bush so dense that the sun's rays sometimes never reached the forest floor.

Despite their fatigue, Thomossene and Suplera quickened their pace, encouraged by the sense of progress. The tears they'd set out with had long been forgotten, replaced by beads of sweat, and feelings of dread swapped for the desire to get things over with.

All of a sudden something came leaping out of the bush and blocked the path before them. It was a *mwanapatche*, his dwarfed body hidden by a buffalo hide that smelled so foul it could only have been killed a few days ago. Without offering any kind of greeting, the *mwanapatche* approached them in an aggressive and unfriendly manner.

'Where were you when you first saw me?'

'Right here, just now!' Thomossene replied, innocently. The *mwanapatche* promptly pulled a large machete from his belt and charged at Thomossene.

'No, wait!' Suplera yelled in desperation, 'We saw you from very far away!' The *mwanapatche* stopped in his tracks and put his machete away.

'In that case you may continue your journey,' he said. 'But you, man, never repeat what you just said if you cross paths with someone of my stature.' Then, just as fast as he'd appeared, he disappeared into the undergrowth.

Thomossene stood there stunned, still too much in shock about having been attacked to even try to comprehend what had just happened. He did not know that *mwanapatches* felt insulted if someone of regular height said they'd only noticed them at close quarters. Even if you were only alerted to their presence by them asking you the question, you had always to answer that you were very far away, for this made them feel as tall and proud as any man. This was common knowledge in the mountains, less so in Sena, though some people knew. Thankfully Suplera was one of them, for her quick thinking had saved her husband from certain death. It was a reminder that they needed to be extra careful now that they were entering the forest.

They walked on for several hours and outcrops began to appear amidst the trees, a sign that they were coming into the foothills of the mountains. After a while, with the sun having set for the day, they came across a cabin in a clearing. A man of advanced age stood outside tending to a herd of goats. He looked nothing like a *mwanapatche* and so they greeted him and asked him if he knew where N'tchira lived. The man's jaw dropped when they said this and he went back to feeding his goats, pretending he hadn't heard them. They asked again and this time he spun around like he'd stood on an ant's nest.

'Holy god, do you not know who N'tchira is?' the old man said. 'I advise you to go back to wherever you came from right now for I have never met a single human being who has appeared before him and lived to tell the tale. Go home, my friends!'

'We cannot go home!' Suplera pleaded. 'We have good reason to want to see him. Only he can bring us back what we've lost!'

'My children, my children! This man you seek is no ordinary being and he will not allow himself to be seen by ordinary people. I say this knowingly for I, and it pains me to say it, am the only living being to have ever met him. Go home, my children!'

'No!' Thomossene insisted. 'We cannot go home. We have to meet him, even if that means going to hell itself!'

The old man fixed them with an intense stare. He saw the determination in their eyes, a reflexion of the grief and resolve that was driving them on. He seemed to pity them and he gestured for them to enter his cabin.

The place was empty aside from a few bits of broken rock and kindling but a fire crackled away at the centre of the room and offered welcome warmth. The visitors from Sena were finding that dusk in the mountains brought a biting cold. They sat down on a leopard skin mat and looked at their host on the other side of the fire, his rugged face testimony to a long and hard life spent in the mountains.

'Woman, please, take your baby from your chest and lay it down to rest,' he said.

It was not a baby, of course, but Suplera did not want the man to know this and so she kept the inert bundle held to her breast. Tears poured uncontrollably from her eyes, however, and Thomossene felt compelled to tell the stranger their story and speak of the torment that was eating away at their souls.

'This is why we beg you to tell us how to find N'tchira,' he concluded. 'Please help us!'

'Very well, my children, very well!' said the old man. 'The story you have told me is most moving, so pay attention. Behind my cabin there is a trail that will lead you all the way to N'tchira. But remember, you will face many challenges along the way, challenges you must overcome if you are to meet him. And I will say more: be brave and never lose heart, for N'tchira will not allow himself to be seen by just anyone. Remember that the trail leads right into his house and he never leaves home, so visitors must go inside to see him. And last but not least: if you do meet him, please, my children, do whatever he says and follow his every instruction, for your own good and the good of your daughter, who, I do believe, is still alive. Now go. Travel well!'

The old man led them out of his cabin and pointed to the trail. They thanked him and set off, determined to make inroads before nightfall. But as soon as they left the clearing it became instantly dark, as if a lamp had been blown out. They pressed on, penetrating deeper into the bush and trying not to lose sight of the trail, which Thomossene concluded must have been opened up by antelopes, for there were plenty of them in the mountains. He did not share this observation with Suplera and in fact not a word of conversation passed between them. There was nothing really to say; if this was the sacrifice they had to make to get their daughter back, then they would make it, for she had lit up their lives just as she'd lit up men's hearts from Murraça to Caia to Chupanga and Cheringoma.

It had been a long and hot day and they both felt utterly spent when the path came to a shallow stream. Before they'd had a chance to cross, a strange sight reached them through the twilight. Right there, floating in the middle of the stream, was a fire. Thomossene and Suplera frowned at one another before kneeling down to get a closer look. Four sticks stood crisscrossed and upright with flames at their centre, like a campfire, but on water.

'Who are you?'

The voice came from the water too, from somewhere near the fire.

'Leave me alone,' said the voice, grumpily. 'Let me cook my dinner in peace!'

Thomossene and Suplera were left dumbstruck. Both of them had heard the voice quite clearly, but there appeared to be no one there. All they could see were the flames of the floating fire, which had come to a halt right in front of them, resistant to the current.

Thomossene suddenly started clapping his hands. 'Mambo!' he said, 'It is us, your children, and we humbly ask you to let us pass. Hear our pleas, Mambo, and feel our sadness. You are great, Mambo!'

When he'd finished speaking, he stopped clapping and stood up. The fire began to slip away in the current. Thomossene and Suplera looked at one another and then quickly paddled across the stream. Once they were on the other side, Thomossene took to his knees again and resumed his clapping. 'Thank you, Mambo. You are great!'

He stood up, pleased to have proven himself well-versed in the ways of the mountain spirits and to have redeemed himself in his wife's eyes after his misstep with the *mwanapatche*. He and Suplera watched as the fire floated back upstream to where they'd first seen it, then they set off walking again.

They pushed on as much as they could but the trail looked like it might go on for ever and the night darkness was now real, with only a handful of stars visible through the forest canopy. They were both ready to collapse and when they came upon a leafy panga-panga tree at the side of the track, they decided to stop and make camp under it. They would continue their journey with their energies restored the next morning.

They gathered kindling and made a fire, though it made for an awkward reminder of the strange business at the stream. But they relished the warmth and they needed the flames to ward off wild animals, for who knew what beasts roamed the forest at night.

Lions, as it turned out. Thomossene and Suplera were woken by their roar and found five pairs fanned out around them. They were all big and strong and the last flickers of the fire lit up their sharp teeth. Thomossene and Suplera huddled together, trembling with fear. Suplera felt particularly torn, caught between the instinct to run and the need to hold on to the dead cat at her chest.

'Do something!' she hissed at her husband. Thomossene, sensing that the circle was closing in, summoned all the strength he could muster and said: 'Akhulo, we are your children! We beg for your mercy, oh Akhulo! Once again, it is us, Akhulo, your children!'

His words seemed to have no effect. The lions continued to snarl and bare their teeth and Suplera wondered if she might die of fright before she was eaten. But then the cats gradually withdrew, and though they didn't go far, they settled down and stopped roaring. They remained uncomfortably close and they seemed very alert, almost as if they were watching over Thomossene and Suplera to make sure no other animals bothered them in the night. Still, Thomossene and Suplera found it hard to relax and if they hadn't been so exhausted they surely wouldn't have fallen asleep.

They woke to feel the sun's rays beating on their eyelids, but when they opened them the lions were gone. The fire had gone out and all was quiet aside from the occasional call from a turtledove. In the brightness of day the trail was clearly visible and burrowed on into the bush. They got up and set off once more.

The track began to climb steadily and before long they found themselves looking down over the treetops. They were making good progress when the path turned a corner and they found a large boulder blocking their way. There was no way round it and no getting over it, indeed it seemed to be wedged into the mountain rock.

'It looks like we've reached the end of the trail,' Thomossene sighed, 'and with it the end of our journey.'

'What are we going to do then?'

Thomossene was quiet for a moment. 'We have no choice but to wait,' he finally said. 'Remember we were told to be patient and brave? Well that's what we'll be, patient. We'll make camp here.'

No sooner had he finished speaking than a man stepped out from the bush. He was of advanced age and a somewhat untidy appearance, and he moved with the aid of a walking stick. He hobbled up to them and stared, taking each of them in and not blinking once. Indeed his lack of blinking caused them both to start blinking excessively themselves. He had a sort of twinkle in his eye but he was so old they worried his skeleton might fall apart at any moment.

'What brings you here, my children?' he said very haltingly, spelling out each word. The couple turned to one another. Where had he come from, this old man, living all on his own in the depths of a dangerous jungle?

'Akhulo, we are looking for N'tchira!' said Thomossene. 'Do you happen to know where we might find him?'

'Why are you looking for him?' the old man asked, clearly surprised. So Thomossene told him the whole story, right from the start, explaining about the Zambeze and how every year people drowned when it flooded and that the spirits of those people lived at the bottom of the river and were forever interfering in the lives of the living.

'I can only imagine your distress,' said the old man. 'But

I must also advise you to give up on your mission. Go home, my children, before you regret it!'

'No, we cannot!' replied Thomossene.

The old man looked at him and saw the stubbornness in his face. 'Then good luck!' he said, and with that he disappeared back to wherever he'd come from.

The couple stood there for a moment feeling utterly bewildered.

'Let's look for firewood, dear,' Thomossene eventually said, to take their mind off what had just happened as much as anything else. 'We'll spend the night right here!'

It was true that night would soon be drawing in and they'd need to make a fire to keep warm. They assembled a good pile of wood and were just about to light it when another figure came out from a nearby thicket. And then another. Like their earlier visitor, these two men were very old and used walking sticks.

'What are you doing here?' said one of the men. 'Where have you come from?'

'We've come from a long way away,' said Thomossene. Then, once again, using as few words as possible this time, he explained what had brought them to the mountain. When he'd finished, he asked the men if they knew where a witch called N'tchira lived.

'Ah, you've come to see N'tchira!' exclaimed the second of the two men. 'My children, go home, for the man you seek is not just anyone, nor will he be seen by just anyone.'

'But Akhulo, we cannot turn back now,' Thomossene pleaded.

'In that case, we wish you luck!' the two men replied in

unison. Then they turned around and headed off back into the bush. Thomossene and Suplera went back to setting up their fire, for they were starting to get used to inexplicable things happening.

Night moved definitively in, and though the sky was full of stars, the forest was dense and dark around them. The fire crackled as it did battle with the cold that populated the Gorongoza mountains. The boulder stood quiet and the air remained still. Only the occasional howl of some wild animal or other broke the bleak peace.

The sun's rays had yet to breach the forest when they woke. They rubbed their eyes and sat up, and then they rubbed them again because they could not believe what they were seeing: the boulder was gone and in its place was the opening to a cave.

They looked around as if the boulder might have rolled somewhere. But it had vanished and the trail they'd been following led straight into the cave. They could not see far inside but an indecipherable sound echoed from within its depths. It was very distant and there was something eerie about it, for it resembled the beat of a drum or a heart and yet it seemed not to be of this earth. Whatever it was, it had them in its thrall and not even the morning birdsong could distract them from it.

They both knew they had to follow the trail to its end if they wanted to meet N'tchira and they'd said they'd follow it to hell if necessary. They'd met mouths that had told them to be brave and others that had told them to give up and go home. Suplera, clutching a bundle that was both the source of their suffering and the reason why they were deep inside the

Gorongoza mountains, stood up and went over to the entrance to the cave. She hesitated at the threshold for a moment and then led the way in.

X

THE N'TCHIRA

The darkness in the cave was different to the kind of darkness they knew, the darkness of night. Strange shapes lurked in the shadows on either side of the track and there was a tiny bright spot up ahead. The trail appeared to be leading towards it without ever getting any closer. The deeper they went into the cave, the louder was the hypnotic sound, louder and yet more indecipherable. Shapes leapt from one side of the path to the other, behind them one minute, in front of them the next. Then a huge cry ripped through the darkness and repeated itself dozens of times as it bounced off the walls. It was so loud it could easily have burst their eardrums and they flung themselves to the ground. Neither of them had ever heard a sound like it before, nor ever heard such a sound described by anyone, for it was like the cry of an animal or a bird, just not one that had ever inhabited the face of the earth. Then came laughter, deep, uncontrollable laughter, echoing around the cavern, now near, then far. With fear coursing through their veins, they forced themselves up, shaken but determined, and they resumed their shuffling through the damp gravel towards the bright spot. They seemed finally to be getting closer and it began to twinkle in a variety of colours, albeit unfamiliar colours, colours they'd never seen before, and the closer they got, the quicker it changed colour. Then after a few more steps, the spot stopped moving and ceased to change colour. It stood static in their path and the laughter started up again. They took a step to the right and the spot moved to block them; they took a step left and it blocked them again. They had to keep following the trail, which meant they had to get past the spot. But how?

Then suddenly the spot was gone as the whole cave flooded with light. The laughing stopped, there was no more movement in the shadows. Thomossene and Suplera froze as they looked around them and saw there were skulls everywhere. Some were human, some belonged to birds and other animals they recognised, others to beings they'd surely never seen before. There were skulls on the ground, skulls stacked up against the walls, skulls placed on ledges high up where they seemed to have been since time immemorial. They were in some sort of catacomb and the scene was all the more macabre for the dramatic lighting, though where it had come from they did not know. They looked up but saw no opening in the cave roof through which sunlight could enter, indeed the glare didn't seem to be coming from any particular place or direction, it was everywhere. They had the strong sense of having entered, if not the devil's lair, then the lair of another creature from hell.

The trail had petered out and they realised they had reached its end. They were in a giant cavern and when they finally looked straight ahead they saw that right in the centre of the space was a chest. It was carved from stone and had engravings down its sides, diabolical images and symbols that Thomossene and Suplera thought looked vaguely familiar. Indeed they'd seen them before, on a girl's body, for they were the same images and symbols that Mbemba had tattooed on her breasts and belly. Before they'd had a chance to think about what this might mean, their eyes noticed that there was something floating above the chest. Strips of various animal pelts had been plaited into a ponytail and attached to a handle made of multicoloured beads. It was, of course, a giant *n'tchira*.

Was this what they'd come all this way to see? They'd imagined N'tchira would be a witch named after a *n'tchira*, not an actual *n'tchira*. But then they remembered they'd been told that N'tchira would not be seen by just anyone. Was the witch there but they couldn't see him?

They puzzled over these questions and more as they stood watching the *n'tchira* swing slowly back and forth. The quiet in the cave was absolute, as if in reverence for the chest and the wand and the dead whose skulls filled the cavern. But then that silence was shattered as the *n'tchira* began to rattle and spit with fire. Thomossene and Suplera fell to the ground, cowering, terrified.

Nothing else happened and they slowly regained their composure. They adopted kneeling positions and Suplera took the dead cat from her arms and laid it out in front of her, as if in offering. Then they bowed towards the strange chest and wand and started to clap.

'Mbuia N'tchira, it is us, your children!' said Thomossene. 'We have come to you because only you can help us!'

They went on clapping their hands and each clap became louder as it echoed around the cavern. Then a strong wind blew into the cavern and put the wand's flames out. And then the lid of the chest began to open.

'My children, I know what afflicts you!' bellowed a deep voice. 'I know why you are here and I will take care of your problem, but you must be patient and brave. First unwrap the animal you have brought for me and place it beside the chest!'

The voice seemed to come from inside the chest, though the box looked too small for anyone to fit inside. Wherever it was coming from, it was authoritative and so they obeyed. They unwrapped the dead cat together and were surprised to see it showed no signs of decomposition and gave off no kind of rotting smell. It seemed not to have changed at all since they'd dug it up from Tchanaze's grave almost a week ago.

Suplera stood up and placed the cat's corpse before the trunk, then quickly knelt back down. The *n'tchira* floated over to the dead animal and began to spark and flame again. Then it moved away and the dead cat turned a deep orange, as if it were being roasted, though there was no smell of cooking meat.

'Thomossene!' said the voice of N'tchira, great warlock of the Gorongoza mountains. 'I command you to pick the cat up the moment my home turns to darkness.'

Right on cue, the light vanished from the cavern and they were surrounded by pitch black again. The only thing they could see was the red-hot glow of the dead cat and a whiter light that came out of the chest.

'Now!' thundered the voice. Thomossene got to his feet hesitantly and moved forward. He was sweating profusely, from nerves rather than the heat of the flames, unsure quite what he was expected to do. How was he supposed to pick up something from a burning fire?

'Pick it up, man!' boomed the voice. 'Those who seek my wisdom must be brave and never lose heart. Pick it up, under penalty of the direst of punishments!'

Thomossene steeled himself and reached into the orange glow. Sparks spat at him but he kept stretching out his hands until they were within touching distance of the cat. Then he lunged forward and reached for it, bracing himself for fierce heat and burnt skin. But he met with the opposite: the cat was as cold and solid as a block of ice.

Light suddenly flooded the cave again and the embers disappeared. Thomossene looked down and saw that what he held in his hands was no longer a cat's corpse but a stick. It appeared to have been carved from a dark wood and bore no traces of the animal or the fire.

'Very good, Thomossene! How brave you are!' came the voice from the chest, its tone slightly mocking. 'Now take that baton out to the entrance of my home and stick it in the neck of whatever you find there. Your wife stays here with me.'

Thomossene hesitated.

'Come on, man!' yelled the voice. 'If you emerge victorious, bring back the spoils of war!'

Thomossene exchanged looks with Suplera and set off walking. Despite having had a sudden blast of cold, he was still sweating heavily. He did not need to follow a bright spot this time for the cave was well lit. Where was the light coming from? He decided it was best not to try to understand anything.

He walked purposefully, and able to see where he was going, soon reached the cave entrance. He stepped outside and the instant he did so he was under attack. A strange beast was charging at him, flames spewing from its mouth, eyes and nostrils. It had a lion's head but it was not a lion, for it had a crocodile's tail, though it was not a crocodile either. It had four legs, each one different: one was a lion's and one was a crocodile's, but there was also a caveman's foot and a horse's hoof. There was a bird's crest on top of the lion's head, and a thick horse's mane. In other words, it was a being like none Thomossene had ever seen before.

The animal rammed into him and knocked him to the ground. Thomossene got quickly back to his feet but he'd dropped the baton and there was no time to pick it up because the beast was coming for him again. It charged him, furiously breathing out fire and steam, but Thomossene swerved and swooped down to recover the baton. The animal turned and charged again but Thomossene stood his ground this time, holding the baton high in his right hand. Then, when the animal was practically upon him, he swayed to the side, swivelled and plunged the baton into the back of its neck. Man and beast fell to the ground, landing side by side. Thomossene scrambled to his feet ready to resume battle, but the strange animal had disappeared. In the space where it had fallen there was now a shiny green stone. Thomossene picked it up and rushed back into the cave.

He found the cavern in total silence. Suplera was still kneeling in worship and the *n'tchira* was still hovering over the chest. Thomossene thought about trying to sneak a look inside as he went past but the voice spoke to him before he had the chance.

'Well done, my child, well done! Now take that little stone to Kumalolo where you will be told what to do next to get your daughter back. But pay attention: you must carry the stone closed in your right fist and never open it. No matter what happens, do not open that fist until you've reached Kumalolo. Now go and never come back! I have spoken.'

The lid of the chest slowly began to close. But then it stopped halfway and the voice boomed out again: 'Oh, and Suplera, if anything strange happens on the journey home, untie your *dhanda* as fast as you can!'

With that the lid slammed shut. The cavern was plunged back into darkness and the indecipherable shadows reappeared, darting across the cave walls as if in some sinister dance. Voices from beyond the grave began to emerge, muttering at first, then cackling. The bright spot had returned and Thomossene and Suplera realised they would have to follow it again, trust it to guide them to the exit. They left the cavern and the catacomb and walked slowly down the trail, trying to block out the voices and shadows around them and focus only on the spot. Suplera was relieved to be able to move freely but

Thomossene now had a stone in his fist and their progress was slow, until eventually the spot vanished, lost in the daylight of the outside world.

XI

RETURNING TO SENA

Rather than follow one particular trail, they took a number of side paths as they made their way down the mountain. These paths had been made by a variety of different animal species and cut through the jungle according to their own criteria. Sometimes they even doubled back on themselves but Thomossene and Suplera didn't mind so long as they headed downwards. They knew that if they kept moving towards the rising sun, they were on their way home.

They walked to a backdrop of monkey calls but not a word left their own mouths. The sense of anguish that had gripped their faces on the way had been replaced by a look of mild triumph as they returned. They'd survived their experience with N'tchira and won the first battle in their quest to bring their daughter home. They knew further challenges would follow but they'd proven themselves patient and brave and there could be no doubting their determination. They felt responsibility too, towards their daughter, first and foremost, but also towards everyone else, for Tchanaze had fostered people's dreams and been used as a conduit by good spirits. Without her, who would herald bumper harvests of sorghum, corn and millet?

Such thoughts occupied their minds when a figure stepped out onto the path before them. Up in the treetops monkeys leapt from branch to branch and a fierce sun beat down on their heads. But at ground level the man before them barely reached their knees. He walked purposefully up to Thomossene and went to shake his hand.

'Greetings. Where were you when you first saw me?'

It was a *mwanapatche*.

'Careful!' yelled Suplera.

'Very far away!' said Thomossene, pleased with himself.

But that wasn't what Suplera had meant with her warning. She'd noticed Thomossene stretching out an arm to greet the *mwanapatche* and now she leapt at him and tried to force his hand shut. But she was too late and Thomossene and the *mwanapatche* shook hands. In a flash, they both turned into gorillas and went bounding off into the bush.

Suplera stood there stunned. Her husband had just turned into a gorilla. Thomossene was gone, perhaps no longer existed. The shiny stone was gone too, the stone they were supposed to take to Kumalolo to win their daughter back. She sunk to the ground and started to cry.

Then she remembered the last thing N'tchira had said to her. She reached for her *dhanda* and tossed it into the bushes. When she looked up, she could not believe her eyes: sitting opposite her on a rock was Thomossene, his right hand clamped shut. Behind him, the *mwanapatche* ran away into the forest.

'Never do that again!' she said, desperately pleased to see her husband but angry at his carelessness. 'Never, you hear me?'

'Sorry, dear wife, I forgot,' he said. 'But it's all over now. We should go.'

He jumped off the rock, picked her up and led them away. They both knew there was no point in dwelling on what had happened, in trying to understand the ways of the spirit world. They still had several days' walk ahead of them and no doubt other strange things would occur.

Sure enough, a few days later, with the mountain peaks now some distance behind them, they were following a path through the forest when they came upon a stream. It was mid-afternoon and they were hot and thirsty and the water looked crystal clear. But when they got closer, they realised it gave off a strong sulphuric smell. Not only that, the water at the stream's edge was simmering and sending clouds of steam up into the trees. Where the steam reached the canopy, it condensed into large droplets, which eventually fell off the leaves and caused a loud splash. Thomossene and Suplera could see the whole cycle unfold right before their eyes.

Despite the vaporising, grass grew tall and verdant at

the edge of the stream and there were many bright flowers in a variety of colours. The only sound was the sizzle of the water and the splash of falling drops. There was no birdsong, no wolves howling in the distance and no sign of any other animals nearby. It was as if they'd come upon another world, one so full of charm and mystery that it seemed unreal and made them feel uneasy. They sat down, enchanted but also unsure of how to get across. The steam was everywhere, which made it hard to see, and they began to feel wet from the moisture in the air and the droplets that fell on their heads.

Then something appeared to them through the dense vapour. In the middle of the stream was a chest. It looked just like the one in the cavern and it was also made of stone, though it was floating on the surface of the water. Its sides were covered in the same strange images and symbols, though they appeared to be burning. But aside from the burning, the chest looked identical to the one they'd seen in N'tchira's cave and they'd have been prepared to swear on the lives of their dead ancestors that it was one and the same.

Half expecting N'tchira's voice to address them, they both looked away, perhaps sensing that averting their eyes was the best way to avoid losing their minds. But they'd seen enough to know that the chest and its carvings were not of this world. The craftsmanship of humankind was not easily mistaken for the devil's handiwork and this chest, like N'tchira's, bore all the hallmarks of having been made in the workshops of hell.

Thomossene forced himself to look up to see if there was a hovering wand, but there wasn't. He then took to his knees and bowed in veneration of the spirits that he sensed were all around them and in anticipation of whatever satanic revelation the trunk was about to make. Unthinkingly he raised his hands to clap, at which point Suplera pounced on him. They struggled, rolling around on the damp grass until the woman's strength imposed itself.

'No!' she cried, straddling him and pinning his closed hand to the ground. 'You cannot open it! Don't forget what you've got in that hand!'

Thomossene realised the mistake he'd been about to make. He was under express orders not to open his hand until they reached Kumalolo and he'd almost opened it for a second time.

'Oh Suplera, thank you! Forgive me, dear wife!' he said, his voice muffled. 'It's true, I'd forgotten my instructions.'

She got off him and they both sat on their knees. Together they bowed before the chest but this time Suplera took the lead.

'Akhulo, it is us, your children!' she said, sobbing and clapping her hands as her husband looked on admiringly. 'We ask that you kindly let us pass, for you are Mbuia. Remember that we've come from far and have suffered a lot!'

She spoke more in hope than expectation but occult forces heard her and the steam began to clear. The intensity of the simmering at the stream's edge slowed too and the water became still and silent. Even the sulphurous smell disappeared. They looked up to where the chest was but it had gone. The stream's crystalline waters slipped on by as if the whole thing had been a mirage. The water did not look deep and the current was gentle so they dipped their toes in and found the water to be cool. Without further ado, they waded swiftly across and stepped up onto the bank on the other side. As soon as they'd done so, the steam reappeared. They turned to see the water bubbling again, vapours floating up to the trees and condensing on the branches. The sulphuric smell came back and there in the middle of the stream was the floating chest.

Thomossene and Suplera hurried away. They'd seen enough to know they'd come upon a place that was special to the spirit world. The souls of invisible beings, long dead, had made it their bathing area. Spirits good and bad took the waters here, cleansed themselves and washed away the dust and misery of the tombs. It was not a place for the living to be and Thomossene and Suplera were anxious to get away from it as quickly as possible. Indeed they were anxious to leave the forest behind and return to the relative safety of the plains.

A few days later, Sena finally appeared on the horizon. A cross between a hamlet and a village, it was a peaceful settlement inhabited by men and women and virgin maidens too, some of whom had skin that glowed, tattoos that dazzled and beads that jingled. As they passed the first houses, the people inside peered out to see if they'd brought Tchanaze back with them. A lot of people had expected they would because they knew she hadn't been buried. But all they saw was Thomossene walking along with his right fist clenched tight and Suplera dragging her feet behind him.

The villagers were curious though, and as Thomossene and Suplera wound their way home, faces appeared at windows and doors. Word spread and travelled on the four winds, and soon everyone in Sena, Mutarara and Dona Ana, and even as far away as Magagade and Murraça, knew that the couple had returned but without Tchanaze.

By the time they reached their hut, a crowd had gathered

outside the door. Farença and Mbemba were there, the root cause of the whole affair, though only they knew this. Some neighbours cried out 'welcome home' or 'you were missed', others rushed forward to offer hugs and handshakes, handshakes that were, of course, declined. But underneath the pleasantries, everyone basically wanted to know the same things: what had happened to them in Gorongoza? What was the witch they'd gone to see like? Was N'tchira old, very old or surprisingly young? Was he frightening, terrifying or the devil himself?

Thomossene and Suplera said nothing. For a start, they did not know how to explain what N'tchira was like. All they knew was that they never wanted to see him again, if they had in fact seen him; it was all very confusing.

Campira had also got word of the couple's return, though unlike everyone else he was informed of it by his dearly departed grandfather in a dream, and unlike everyone else he wanted to protect them rather than quiz them. He pushed through the crowd and led them into their house. He spoke to them for a moment and told them to get some rest, then he went back outside to address the crowd.

'My friends, people of Sena! As you all know, Thomossene and his wife have just got back from a long journey and they need to rest. I ask you to all go home and wait until tomorrow when you will be able to greet them properly. I have spoken!'

As the only healer in the village and the only person capable of overseeing funeral ceremonies, for which there was some demand, Campira was highly respected and no little feared. And so, although the villagers were frustrated by what he said, they did as he asked. After all, tomorrow would come soon enough and they would find out everything then.

What they did not know was that Campira had arranged to come for Thomossene and Suplera later that night and take them straight to Kumalolo.

XII

KUMALOLO ONCE AGAIN

Thomossene, Suplera and Campira reached Kumalolo as the sun's first rays spread from the east of the valley across the great river and the spirits of the drowned. Just as on previous visits, the warlock was standing at the door of his hut when they arrived. He offered them no smile and not the merest hint of a welcome. He just stood there, a skeletal, bony figure adorned with necklaces of the kind no human had ever worn and tattoos that were clearly the markings of the devil. According to local lore, Tchinai, the dead man whose body the warlock now inhabited, had had no such craters in his own skin.

Phanga had known they were coming for he'd been alerted

to it while dreaming of his kin. Now he stood there staring at them, looking them up and down, glaring as if in rebuke or astonishment. His eyes travelled down to Thomossene's right hand, clenched tight in a fist. Then, without saying a word or responding to their greetings, he went into his cabin and slammed the door shut.

'Relax,' said Campira, noticing how crestfallen the couple seemed. 'He has simply retired to perform his morning ceremonies and to enter into dialogue with the deceased. These are his daily rituals! We must wait. He'll see us when he's ready.'

And so they stood and waited. They soon heard a tremendous din coming from inside the hut, as if a vicious fight had broken out. A spine-tingling wail went up followed by the sound of a human body crashing to the floor. There was lots of thrashing around and then the whole cabin began to shake, he seemed to be hurling himself against the walls. The wailing made way for an animal-like howl and then the repetitive sound of a head hammering on the wall. The three visitors exchanged nervous looks. Daily rituals they may have been, but they were still extremely sinister and strange.

Then there was silence, absolute silence. After a while, they heard laboured, deep breaths, but still they waited, until finally the door creaked open and the shadowy figure of a man who clearly consorted with demons appeared. Blood dripped from his lips and he had bruises all over his body. Whatever fight he'd just been in, he appeared to have lost.

'Come in!' he yelled, wiping the blood from his lips with the back of his hand. 'I said come in!'

He promptly turned his back on them and disappeared

inside the hut. They looked at one another uncertainly, for the warlock had still yet to acknowledge them or give any indication he recognised who they were. But they followed him in and stood by the door to await further instruction. Meanwhile, the great witch slipped into his ceremonial gown, mindless of their presence. He piled more beads on top of the ones he already had on and then grabbed a tail, though to what animal it had once belonged they could not say, perhaps several. He began his ritual, issuing damnations and waving his tail-wand around. Then he screamed, sending a shudder through Thomossene and Suplera. Even Campira, though he was used to such things and a master of magic and witchcraft himself, was given a fright, for it was a scream surely tuned to the wavelength of Satan himself. The warlock then collapsed to the floor and began writhing around, rolling from one side of the room to the other and then banging his head against the wall again, causing more blood to pour from his mouth. Phanga had been a mysterious character from the moment they'd met him, but now, as he flailed around the room, he truly seemed to be possessed by the devil.

Eventually he fell to the floor and lay there in a heap, still and silent, but for his panting. After a while he got up, moving very slowly, and sat down in front of them. He wiped the blood from his chin with his free hand.

'Greetings!' he said. But it was not him speaking. The voice that came out of his mouth was tired and hesitant and female. 'My name is Nhantete, Mbemba's great grandmother. We spoke before, the last time you visited!'

From within the warlock's eyes, the woman called Nhantete gave Thomossene and Suplera a hard stare. Then she pointed one of Phanga's fingers at them.

'I know you met the man I told you about and I know what you've brought back with you.'

'Can I open my hand now?' asked Thomossene. He was tired of clenching his fist, he'd been doing it for days.

'No!' she said. 'I only came to tell that you must do as my dear friend says. He will tell you how to get your daughter back. I know because I know who gave her *n'fúcua*.'

Her voice fell silent and was soon replaced by heavy panting. Then the howling and screaming started up again and the warlock collapsed to the floor and began rolling and thrashing around the hut. As he rubbed his face against the walls the blood, which had dried on his lips, began to flow from his mouth again and trickle down his neck. Thomossene and Suplera looked on, overwhelmed by feelings of sadness, pity and fear. It was disturbing to see, up close and personal, just how much control the lost souls of the Zambeze had over human skeletons, the power they had to manipulate and abuse spent bodies. Even Campira was moved for it was a particularly macabre spectacle.

The troubling scene lasted for several minutes, until the warlock's movements finally slowed and he slumped to the floor. Blood from his mouth and the cuts he had all over his body caused pools of red gloop to form in the earth floor. He looked dead but they knew he was just asleep because he began to snore. And what a strange snoring it was! It was so thunderously loud that the whole cabin shook upon every breath. Campira couldn't help but smile in admiration for in all his many years of witchcraft he had never encountered anything like this. There was no doubt about it, they were in the presence of a fugitive from hell.

Campira turned to face Thomossene and Suplera.

'According to my ancestors, we have to sit here and wait until dawn tomorrow, for our host will remain like this until then,' said Campira. 'Please be patient and remain seated just as you are.'

Thomossene and Suplera listened to the healer in astonishment. They had been told repeatedly that they'd need to be patient and brave, and so it was proving. But what else could they do besides wait? So they waited.

They sat there all day and all night waiting for Phanga to stir, a man they thought was the devil incarnate but who was, for now, no more than a heap of bones on a wet floor. They kept still and quiet and tried to get some sleep themselves. Indeed they had all three nodded off when they were woken by the warlock springing to his feet.

'Yhááauuu! Yhááauuu!' he yelled in a way that only he knew how. He began moving around in a confined circle with the tail held out before him. 'You thought I was dead? I'm here and I'm alive, yhááauuu!'

As the three visitors from Sena came to, they realised that something very strange had happened. The man's body had healed its cuts and bruises and there was not a trace of dried blood on his lips. The warlock had awoken as if renewed. Now he was bouncing around from side to side with a look of great satisfaction on his face. Then, just as suddenly as he'd jumped up, he sat down.

'You, woman, wait outside!' he said to Suplera and he pointed to the door. His voice was firm, so she stood up and left.

The warlock turned to Thomossene. 'Now you, man, divest!'

Thomossene did not understand what he meant.

'Strip, man!' said the warlock. 'But keep your fist closed!'

Thomossene stood up and took off his clothes. While he did so, Phanga went to get a pitcher from the corner of the room. They both sat back down and Phanga poured water from the pitcher into an earthenware pot and then placed the pot in between Thomossene's naked thighs.

'Now pay attention!' he said. 'Put your right hand in the pot. When it is fully immersed you may open it.'

Sitting there stark naked, Thomossene looked at the other two men and then peered inside the pot. It appeared to contain nothing but water, albeit a murky kind of water presumably taken from the mangrove nearby. He stuck his hand in, then nearly pulled it out again in surprise. The water had started to fizz and give off a purplish vapour. He forced himself to keep his hand submerged and soon sparks began to fly, sparks that then turned into flames. His hand was immersed in a pot of boiling water and yet he felt no heat, nor did his skin burn from the flames. In fact, if anything the water felt cold and the flames were like icy tongues licking his arm.

'Now open your hand very slowly,' said the warlock. The flames suddenly disappeared back inside the pot and the steam dissipated. 'That's it, yes!'

The water stopped boiling and went purple, the same colour as the vapour, and then red, blood red.

'Now bathe in the water!' said the warlock. He thrust a mug at Thomossene and gestured for him to get on with it. 'Bathe, man, come on! Take the mug in your right hand!'

Thomossene opened his right hand and saw that the little stone was gone. He picked up the mug and used it to pour the strange liquid over his head and shoulders. Its smell was as unfamiliar to him as it would have been to any man on earth and although it was the colour and consistency of blood, it left no tinge on his skin.

'Enough!' snapped the warlock.

'You can put your clothes back on,' said Campira, who'd been silent and watchful up until then.

'Exactly, my dear Campira,' said the warlock. 'Get dressed and fetch your wife!'

Thomossene did as he was told. Suplera came back in and sat down next to him, facing the man they knew as Phanga but whose real name was unknown to anyone in Sena, Kumalolo, Gorongoza and beyond.

'Now listen carefully! Your daughter was given *n'fúcua* and for this she should have died. The spirits had their fun with her but some of them, three friends in particular, were so taken by her beauty that passions were roused and they decided to keep her alive. When you went to bury her, they switched her body for a cat, but then lost souls escaped from hell swooped in and spirited her away. Do you understand?'

'Yes sir,' they said, though really they did not.

'Good,' he said, bringing the tail he'd been wafting around right up to his nostrils. 'Because now we must rescue her. Follow my instructions very carefully and do whatever my friend, here, tells you to do. He will take this liquid, made from blood, in a flask to Inhangoma where first you, man, and then you, woman, will pour it around the hut where the creature who looks like your daughter lives. Campira will take care of everything else, he knows what to do. Afterwards, bring the girl back to me and I will finish her treatment. Yhááăuuu! Now go, yhááăuuu!'

XIII

BACK TO INHANGOMA

They were back on the other side of the Zambeze again, where word of a beautiful woman who lived in an isolated shack in the reeds continued to spread. Arguments waged over whether such an exquisite woman had ever been born in the valley before, some claiming she was more beautiful than Tchanaze, others that Sena's fair maiden had the edge. Discussions rumbled on into the night, fuelled by fermented drink and drumbeats.

Campira, Thomossene and Suplera had spent the night in Sena, having got back late from Kumalolo. But they rose early, crossed the bridge and were in Mutarara by late morning.

Campira sent Thomossene to get a red cloth with dark patches, for according to his grandfather he would have to wear the same vestments as before if he wanted to find Fineja's house again. What's more, the healer now knew that the woman was possessed by evil spirits from the underworld. These spirits would do everything in their power to stop anyone getting near her, especially anyone sent by Phanga or N'tchira.

Thomossene got back with the cloth in the late afternoon and Campira set off for the riverbank right away. A gentle breeze sent ripples through the reeds and a damp smell rose up from the entrails of the river, the smell of the humus of the shipwrecked and the drowned. There was no sign of a shack anywhere but Campira hadn't expected there to be and instead he sought out the pile of incongruous rocks. He found them just as the sun slipped beneath the horizon, then he walked away from them, ploughing a trail straight through the prickly reeds. When he stopped it was dark. He took off his clothes and changed into the red cloth ready to commune with his spirits and receive their instruction. He crouched down and turned towards where the sun had set. Then he began to evoke his dead ancestors in a monologue that used words of sorcery that only he and his people could understand. There he remained, in a sacrificial pose, until the sun reemerged to touch him with its rays and return him to the land of the living. He came to feeling confident that yet another battle had been won.

It was midday by the time he got back to the village. Thomossene and Suplera were pleased to see him and anxious to get going. They wanted to know if he'd seen Fineja. They wanted news.

'Get ready, we'll be heading for the river when night falls!'

was all Campira would say. They were left to guess at the rest from the cheerful expression on his face. This reassured them, for they detected signs of triumph, but they would have done whatever he said anyway for they had unlimited faith in him. When all was said and done, Campira and other practitioners of the dark arts commanded everyone's respect, in Sena, Mutarara and even Kumalolo, for they clearly got great pleasure from performing their craft, and that craft involved conducting regular conversations with the dead.

As soon as night fell, Campira, Thomossene and Suplera set off for the mangroves down by the river. As they made their way out of the village, they left behind the last flickers of light seen through the walls of village huts, which in Mutarara, as elsewhere in the valley, were made from clay and cane or clay and bamboo, topped with thatched roofs of sedge. The trio made their way through the dark to where the pile of stones had been but where there was now a little house. They glimpsed flashes of light through cracks in the walls here too, and there was the sound of someone singing. The singing was soft but it reached them clearly in the quiet of the night and the couple immediately recognised the melody, for they'd heard it many times before. They recognised the timbre of the voice too, for it was the voice of their daughter, Tchanaze, the fair maiden who'd died of *n'fúcua*, or so it had been thought. Now it seemed she'd been kept alive and kidnapped by spirits escaped from hell.

'We'll wait here until she goes to sleep!' said Campira, gesturing for them to sit down in the sedge a short distance from the shack's door. But then the door opened. The woman who claimed to be Fineja stood at the threshold, her chest bare but for her beads, which sparkled under the moonlight. It was an image that appeared to the region's menfolk in dreams and filled their hearts with a rainbow of colours. The girl sat down in the doorway, and still singing, contemplated the stars in the sky. As if by magic or sorcery, her lips seemed to dispel the night breeze. After a minute or two, she stood up and went back inside. She shut the door behind her, put out her lamp and stopped singing.

'She must have gone to bed!' Campira whispered. 'We'll wait for a few more hours.'

And that's what they did. By the time Campira was satisfied that she'd be in a sufficiently deep sleep, it was the middle of the night.

'Suplera, take this flask and pour the liquid around the cabin,' he said. 'Strip naked when you get to the door.'

She took the flask from him, went over to the door and took off her clothes. Then she made her way silently around the outside of the hut, splashing the red potion on the ground. Silence reigned inside the shack, broken only occasionally by a bout of spluttered snoring. When Suplera had completed her task, she got dressed and came back.

'Now you, Thomossene, do exactly the same.'

Thomossene took the flask, deposited his clothes by the door and did just as his wife had done. Then he got dressed again and rejoined the others.

'Now it's my turn,' said Campira. 'Don't go anywhere!'

The healer took the potion and went over to the door. He knelt down and stayed in that position for several minutes, then stood up. He did not strip naked but proceeded to pour the rest of the liquid on the ground in front of the cabin. When the flask was empty, he dug a hole by the door with his hands and buried the flask. After making sure the hole was properly covered, he reached into his pouch and took out his witch's mask and magic tail. Then he put the mask on and went into the hut.

Everything was dark and silent in the room except for the woman's snoring. Campira went over to where she lay and waved the tail in the air above her, wafting it over the full length of her body. He was seeking to banish the evil spirits that had made her their wife and home. Sure enough, after a few minutes, bats and owls began to exit her body. Thomossene and Suplera watched in amazement outside as dozens of them flew out of the window. More and more bats and owls came out of her until it became a constant stream, though they were not in fact bats or owls but malignant spirits, malevolent souls that had taken up residence in her body and used her for their orgies. Now they were fleeing from Campira's powers and from three men who had lost their lives to the river's anger when their canoe had capsized, three friends who had fallen for Tchanaze on her deathbed and decided to save her, only for wicked spirits to steal her away. They urged the healer on and leant him extra strength as he waved his wand relentlessly, sending bats and owls crashing into the hut's walls in their mad rush to escape.

The flow eventually relented, became fitful and then stopped. The healer left the shack, took off his mask and put the tail back in his pouch.

'We can go back to the village now,' he said to Thomossene and Suplera. 'We'll come back this afternoon. We've earned a rest!'

Thomossene and Suplera noticed that his voice, while gruff, was jubilant, though they struggled to share in his delight. They had just watched him expel hundreds of bats and owls from their daughter's body. They'd known he was a healer and that he was esteemed, but it had never occurred to them that his powers of witchcraft might reach such heights. They saw him in a different light now, as a witch rather than Campira, their friend and neighbour. They were now very much afraid of him and they followed him back to the village in silence.

By mid-afternoon they were following him back down to the river again, still silent, still too intimidated to ask him anything. They entered the reeds and saw the cabin immediately, alone in the landscape, isolated from the rest of the village. All they heard was the ripple of reeds in the breeze but then the breeze brought a melody to them, the same one as before, soft and tender, sung in a voice that had set so many hearts aflame, among the living and the dead.

'Tchanaze, come on out!' Campira yelled in an assertive voice. 'Come out, Tchanaze, your parents are here, we've come to take you home!'

Thomossene and Suplera stood there not knowing what to do. Fineja stopped singing and came to the door. She looked out nervously but did not recognise them, could not recognise them. It was quite clear that in her eyes they were all total strangers, unwelcome intruders even. Nevertheless, Suplera went over to her, desperate to take her daughter in her arms, convinced that the girl would surely recognise her own mother. She did not.

'You are mistaken,' she said, 'my name is Fineja!'

Suplera broke down crying and Thomossene stepped

forward. 'Go away!' yelled Fineja. Thomossene reached out a hand, for he could see that the girl was shaking and tense. He took another step forward but it did not have the desired effect. Fineja panicked and took flight, running through the reeds and off into the bush. Thomossene and Suplera stood there stunned, tears pouring from their eyes.

'Stop crying and go back to Sena!' said Campira. 'I will stay here, for I must deliver her to Phanga. But you should go home. I'll come and see you when I get back from Kumalolo.'

He still had that jubilant look on his face, as if everything was going according to plan or just as his people had said it would.

'Go on! Be on your way!' he said and then he disappeared inside the cabin. He came out carrying a flagon of gasoline and proceeded to pour it around the shack and its yard.

'Please, now, move away from the cabin!' he said, speaking to them very sternly. Then he lit the liquid and the cabin went up in flames.

XIV

CAMPIRA AND TCHANAZE IN KUMALOLO

It could take two days or more to get to Kumalolo from Inhangoma depending on the weather and the availability of canoes. Journey times varied especially in the rainy season when river and land routes got blocked and going anywhere became hazardous. This was the period when the waters feasted on the souls of men or women judged to have defied their forebears, deliberately or otherwise. The Zambeze's vengeful streak spread misery and grief and phrases like 'Bulande and his family were taken by the waters', 'Nhamaze drowned in the rapids' and 'Caphesse's canoe went down carrying Chinquita's son' were heard up and down the river. The rain washed away people and homes, chickens and coups, animals and pens, and spread scenes of devastation throughout the valley.

But the rainy season had now passed and Campira and Fineja made good time. He'd found her hiding in the reeds, though he'd had to consult his ancestors first. He'd let his tail-wand guide him through the mangroves and come upon her crouched down in the mud, whimpering.

'Do not flee, Tchanze, I mean you no harm,' he'd said.

'But I am Fineja!' she'd replied through her tears.

'I know!' he'd said and he'd waved his tail over her, causing a few more bats and owls and crows to fly out of her, the last ones to holdout. Then he'd reached out a hand and she'd taken it. She was weak, her mind a mess, but he knew the spirits of her ancestors were now present in her and would help him get her to Kumalolo.

It took them just under two days. Unlike on previous occasions, Phanga wasn't at the door to meet them. The silence surrounding the house was absolute, interrupted only by the sporadic call of animals in the riverbanks. The hut sat lifeless and still, but more than anything, it was Phanga's failure to greet them that puzzled Campira for he knew that the warlock had premonitory dreams whenever visitors were coming. After all, Phanga had escaped from hell and appropriated the body of one of the Zambeze's dead, he had eyes and ears in both worlds.

Campira decided it would be best to wait for Phanga to appear so he looked for somewhere they might sit and rest.

There was a panga-panga tree log in the backyard so he led Fineja over to it and they sat down.

Night fell but without a moon and with no stars shining in the firmament. In the pitch black they sensed the presence of ghostly beings moving back and forth, some in groups, others alone. One such creature of the dark caused a bright light to suddenly shine, then quickly fade away. Another appeared, but likewise faded, and on it went. Campira pulled Fineja, or whoever she was, closer to him but she seemed oblivious to what was happening around them. Her indifference was surprising, though Campira knew the ghosts were just *tchipocos,* manifestations of the dead that came out on dark nights to enjoy the cool breeze and relive some of the pleasures they missed from life. Their silhouettes kept shining and fading, their lights sometimes appearing close and other times far away in a dance that people generally found unnerving. From his many years practising witchcraft, Campira knew which deceased person corresponded to which *tchipoco*, but most people believed them to be spirits who had escaped from hell but lacked the black magic skills to possess a human corpse. Thus they were reduced to flying around and haunting the living by twinkling in the shadows, their light a product of the fires that burned in hell. Nobody had ever glimpsed their faces and so nobody knew what form they took. Some said they were like humans but taller than any tree in Sena, others maintained they were short and white and shaped like hyenas.

While Campira watched them darting about the yard, a light went on in the hut. It filtered through the cracks in the walls and flickered in such a way as to suggest that there was someone moving around inside. The healer rose to his feet, walked over to the door and knocked. Nothing. He peeked inside and saw a lamp flickering in the middle of the room and the body of a man lying on the floor beside it. He squinted a little harder and recognised the body as Phanga, or at least the body that Phanga presently inhabited. From the way he lay, he looked to be in a bad way but Campira could tell from the rise and fall of his chest that he was breathing. Campira knocked again but the body did not stir. Yet if Phanga were asleep then who had lit the lamp? Campira surveyed the room with his eyes, there was no one else there. Presumably the warlock had dreamed of his people and they had woken him for just long enough to light the lamp and scare the *tchipocos* away, for the dead disliked any light that was not their own. Campira went back to where Fineja was still sitting on the log. He sat down and prepared to wait some more, and eventually he fell asleep.

The mysterious glowing beings had gone by the time the two visitors were awoken by Phanga's howling and cursing. He screamed so loudly and with such force that anyone hearing it would have shivered in terror. Then came the sound of him bashing into the walls and stomping on the ground. Campira stood up, took Faneja by the arm and walked her to the door as the sound inside the hut built to an ecstatic crescendo. The noise would have scared any bird or person away, for Phanga's morning prayers were not of this world and nobody of this world would have dreamed of interrupting them, no matter how desperately they needed a consultation. But Campira knew it was simply the warlock's way of communing with his people and summoning the dark forces and wisdom they conveyed to him.

The uproar gradually died down and vanished until all the

two visitors could hear was Phanga's panting. Did this man, who incorporated the body of another and mercilessly threw that body against the wall in his prayers, do so simply because the body was not his own? Nobody knew, not in Kumalolo, much less Mutarara, Caia or anywhere else. The warlock's true sentiments would never be known to the inhabitants of the valley and so they should never attempt to understand or judge him.

Campira stood at the door unsure whether to knock or wait, but he listened to his intuition and waited. He knew that for most witches this moment of silence marked the zenith of the day. It was a time of spiritual unification with those who, many sorghum and corn harvests ago, had left their huts and crops and canoes behind and gone to live in the bottom of the river or the chasm where Satan reigned.

The door burst open and Phanga appeared, his scrawny body decked in ceremonial attire, blood dripping from his mouth and nostrils, cuts and bruises all over his face and body. He looked for all the world like he'd escaped from hell once more. His eyes inspected the two visitors from head to toe and then he smiled, a satanic smile the like of which no living person had ever seen.

'Yhááauu, yhááauu!' he yelled by way of a greeting, 'Come in, yhááauu!'

Campira led them inside and over to a mat in the corner. Phanga shut the door and everyone sat down. The warlock proceeded to stare at them without saying a word.

'This is the young woman from Inhangoma,' Campira said, keen to get things moving.

'I know who she is!' snapped Phanga with characteristic

incivility. 'I saw you when you arrived but my people told me to wait and attend to you today. Where are her parents?'

'They went back to Sena,' said Campira and he proceeded to give a brief explanation of what had happened in Inhangoma.

'Well done, Campira, well done!' said Phanga, nodding in seeming approval, which pleased Campira for he'd understood the warlock to be pathologically incapable of praising another. But then Phanga added: 'The woman is practically unconscious, you've left us with a lot of work to do!'

'Right,' said Campira, his pride deflated.

The warlock got to his feet and gestured for Campira to do the same. 'Yes, there is still a lot of work to be done!' he said and stared at the healer. After a moment or two, Campira realised he was being told to leave. He turned and made for the door.

Alone with the woman, Phanga helped her to lie down on the mat. He ran his tail-wand over her body several times, slowly at first but gradually speeding up. Then he began shaking it vigorously above her chest and almost immediately owls and bats started to come out of her mouth and fly around the room. They were the last of the evil spirits residing inside her, chased away by the power of the warlock, who was an evil spirit himself but much mightier than them and more skilled in the dark arts. He could expel malignant souls from entire villages never mind one woman's body.

'Out! Yhááàuu, out!' Campira heard Phanga's cries from outside and he looked up to see dozens of owls and bats flying out of the window. The healer had thought he'd vanquished the last of the evil spirits from inside her, how wrong he'd been!

'Yhááánu, out!' Phanga went on screaming until the woman seemed to be finally coming to her senses.

'Where am I?' she stuttered, 'What am I doing here?' She babbled some more and writhed around on the mat, but the warlock paid her no attention and went on with his work. Soon human bones started spewing from her body, fingers and thumbs at first, then teeth. He kept on going until they stopped coming and then he put his magical tail away. He lifted the girl up and started to undress her, revealing a body and beads that any man in the valley would have died for, or lived for if they were already dead. When she was as naked as the wind, he got a pitcher of water and poured it over her. It was unlike water from the river, or any other kind of water for that matter, for it was of a colour that no human could identify. He washed her with it and then dried her down using his tail of animal hairs, wringing it out whenever it became too saturated. Tiny fragments of flesh and bone fell to the floor amidst the drips. 'Out! Yhááánu, out!' he kept on screaming, and he kept on cleaning her, drying her and wringing out the tail until no human remains appeared. Then he picked her up and helped her get dressed. She was in a total daze and yielded to Phanga's every movement. Eventually he sat her back down on the mat.

'Campira!' he yelled. 'You may enter!'

The healer went in and looked them both up and down. He stared hard at Phanga, unable to believe the warlock could have extracted so many more things from the woman's body. As far as Campira was concerned, Phanga was surely the devil himself.

'Don't look at me like that, Campira!' Phanga said in a chastening but triumphant tone. 'Pick these bits up and take them to Sena. Burn them and mix the ashes with water, then bathe Thomossene and Suplera with the mixture. Come back here afterwards and I will perform the final treatment. The young lady stays with me for now. Yhááauu, I am Phanga and I have spoken!'

XV

RETURN FROM INHANGOMA

Thomossene and Suplera had returned home with mixed feelings. They'd left Campira contemplating the flames of a cabin he'd set on fire, a cabin in the reeds where a beautiful woman lived, perhaps the most beautiful in all the valley. But seeing their daughter again had not been a comfort, in fact it had filled their hearts with yet more sadness and despair. The girl had fled, and despite all their efforts in Gorongoza, seemed no closer to ever coming home.

But getting back to Sena lifted their spirits. They remembered the melody the girl had been singing and pictured themselves returning to the village one day singing it with her. They had infinite confidence in Campira and they trusted in Phanga and even N'tchira too, whose combined witch's wisdom was more than enough to bring about Tchanaze's return.

They got back to Sena at dusk and found the same faces as last time waiting with the same questions: where had they been? What had they been doing? What was the latest news? Everyone knew they'd gone to Gorongoza with the remains of a dead cat and that the cat had been dug up in place of their daughter's corpse, something that had never happened in Sena before and only the very eldest among them knew of anything even remotely similar having happened anywhere else. Everyone knew of the rumours that a beautiful woman had showed up in Inhangoma and that the woman looked very much like Tchanaze, the fair maiden who had given everyone's lives meaning and set every man's heart aflame.

For these reasons and more, Thomossene and Suplera's approach to the village and progress through it was watched by a parade of inquisitive faces. Was Tchanaze alive or dead? That was the first thing people wanted to know. And if she was dead, who was the woman in Inhangoma? And if she was alive, who had they buried and why had they found a cat's corpse in her place?

A crowd had formed outside their hut and Farença and Mbemba were part of it, of course. They, like everyone else, had heard about the couple's various peregrinations, that Campira was directing operations and that there was a woman in Inhangoma believed to be Tchanaze reincarnated. Such rumours made them nervous, not least because they wanted Tchanaze to remain dead. They'd infected her with *n'fúcua* in order to get rid of her as well as to punish her for stealing the affections of every man in the valley. Their trip to see Mabureza, the treatments they'd subjected themselves to, the drops of potion they'd poured over the girl's grave: all these efforts had been aimed at removing the fair maiden from bewitched men's eyes. But if what people said was true and the couple's mysterious comings and goings were the result of their daughter being found alive, then Farença and Mbemba were in trouble. This had not figured in their plans, Mabureza had not told them to expect it. And so, as soon as word reached them of Thomossene and Suplera's return, they rushed to the couple's house along with everyone else. They needed to know the facts of the matter because if it was confirmed that the woman living in Inhangoma was none other than Tchanaze, then they had to inform Mabureza right away.

Thus they took their place in an expectant crowd. Some couldn't contain their curiosity, others believed they had a god-given right to know the truth, all were left disappointed. Thomossene and Suplera returned people's greetings but said not a word about their trips to anyone.

'Tell us everything,' said Farença, as bold as she dared be. 'We're all desperate to know about your daughter!'

'The trip went well,' said Suplera. 'Campira will give you all the details.'

Farença realised the healer wasn't with them.

'Oh, and where is he?'

'He's following on behind,' said Suplera. 'He'll be back soon.'

'Now if you don't mind,' said Thomossene, 'it's been a long journey and we must get some rest.' He led his wife into their cabin and shut the door.

The crowd stood about frustrated, especially Farença. She sensed Suplera was either downplaying things or hiding something. She looked at her daughter and saw that she, too, was dissatisfied. They decided to join others waiting outside Campira's house in the hope that the healer might soon appear. It helped them that others were as keen for information as they were, though it was a reminder of quite how obsessed with Tchanaze the village was. In any case, they waited in vain, for night fell without any sign of the healer. The crowd began to disperse and Farença and Mbemba went home like everyone else. But unlike everyone else, they went home wondering if it had been revealed to Thomossene and Suplera that they were responsible for Tchanaze's death. This was more than possible, for it was known that the couple had gone to the mountains to see a witch, and if it had been revealed to them, they might seek revenge, meaning Farença and Mbemba had better be on their guard.

Thoughts like these prevented them from sleeping. Feeling restless and a little afraid, they decided to consult a seer in the village. It was too late to go and see Mabureza in Kumalolo but they needed to know the truth to put their minds at rest. They snuck out of their home and made their way to the extreme north of the village, keeping their heads bowed and their *capulanas* pulled over their faces to avoid being recognised. They went to the house of Nhamphandza, a simple healer-seer who had yet to gain the same level of acclaim as other men of his profession. He lived with his wife and children and supported them with his divination work. He wasn't a witch or a sorcerer or even a healer in the true sense of the word, but he could divine the source of people's suffering and recommend someone to go to for a cure. In this he was said to be highly competent.

'Who is it?' asked a male voice when they knocked on the door. They could see light from flames in the fireplace through cracks in the cabin walls.

'It's me, Nhamphandza! Farença!'

They heard movement inside and then footsteps. A bearded man opened the door, his body wrapped in a *capulana*.

'At this hour?' he grumbled, a sleepy look on his face. 'We're all asleep.'

'If we've come at this hour, it's because something's afflicting us. Please see us!'

'Very well,' he said with a sigh, 'come in.'

The fireplace gave off a little light and they could make out a dividing wall, behind which Nhamphandza's wife and children presumably lay fast asleep. He offered them a mat and they sat down.

'Tell me, then, what seems to be the trouble?' he said, taking his place at the opposite end of the mat.

'We're here because we need to know something,' Farença said. 'Or rather we need to know everything, everything that happened to Suplera and her husband on their trip.'

'Why should that interest you?' Nhamphandza asked.

'That's our business!' said Mbemba. 'If you won't tell us, we'll consult someone who will."

Nhamphandza looked at her and saw hatred in her eyes.

'Very well, very well,' he said. 'Let me get my things.'

He stood up and went into the room behind the dividing wall, then reappeared carrying a basket. He sat back down and took out various fragments of sea-turtle shell recovered from the banks of the Zambeze.

'I will consult *n'tsango*,' he said.

'That's why we're here!' said Mbemba, mockery betraying her growing anxiety.

Nhamphandza picked the pieces of turtle shell up, shook them in his hands and threw them on the mat.

'Hã hã! Hã, hâ!' he said. Then he repeated the act and said the same thing: 'Hã hã! Hã hâ!'

He did this several times, gathering in his dice and throwing them on the mat. But he eventually stopped with a shrug.

'No, I'm not seeing anything in particular.' He pointed to the scattered shards. 'You see those two dice there? Well, that one's Thomossene and that one's Suplera. You see? Yhá, there they are coming back from Gorongoza.' He gathered his pieces in and threw them again. 'Hã hã! Yhá! You see? There they are in Inhangoma! Hã hã! Hã hâ! Hã, you see? There's nothing there. Something is being hidden from me. All I can see is them travelling from one place to the other, but what they did there, what happened to them, is carefully hidden.'

He looked up at the two women as if this were all obvious.

'You're saying you can't see anything?' Farença asked.

'Exactly,' replied the seer. 'It's very strange but *n'tsango* does not wish to reveal anything.'

'Try again, Mister Nhamphandza,' said Mbemba, refusing to accept what she was being told. 'Try harder, man!'

The seer obliged and went on trying for a while. He tried to summon the spirits of his dead ancestors but got no help. Then he evoked the spirits of his wife's dead ancestors and still got nothing. Everything was hidden, which was itself a sign of just how powerful the witches Thomossene and Suplera had consulted were. Secrets were carefully sealed and Nhamphandza, a simple seer, could not hope to open them.

'No, it's impossible!' he said. 'It's all concealed and secure. Try another seer, by all means, but there's nothing I can do!'

He gathered up his dice and put them back in the basket.

It was now the middle of the night. The dying light of fireplaces glowed inside huts but otherwise the only light came from the stars in the sky. Another night had fallen over Sena, burying its secrets in darkness and blanketing them in silence. Rather than seek out another seer, mother and daughter headed home. They realised they should probably let some events run their course before doing anything else, not least wait for Campira to return. He'd no doubt be back soon and furnish the village with the information they needed. It was important that they remained calm and didn't overreact or do anything suspicious. They would go to Kumalolo at the appropriate moment and Mabureza would come to their aid.

Or so they tried to tell themselves. But such was their state of unrest that no sooner had they got home than they changed their minds and decided to go and consult another seer after all. There was one who lived some distance away in the opposite direction to Nhamphandza, a solitary fellow who lived on his own and went by the name of Baera. He was a very respected man and was reputed to be a great seer, for he'd managed to predict the future of many things including which years the Zambeze would draw villagers into its entrails.

They walked past houses that no longer gave off any

signs of firelight. Baera's cabin was somewhat removed from the other huts, but it too lay silent and dark. Too anxious to stand on ceremony, they knocked on the door. Nothing. They knocked again, more persistently this time, but still they heard nothing. They knocked again, harder and insistently, because they were agitated and because they felt sure that the seer was home. Baera wasn't the sort of person who went out at night and people often sought his services at this hour.

Their stubbornness was eventually rewarded and they heard the sound of someone moving around. Then footsteps came to the door and a half-asleep man made himself heard: 'Who the hell is it?' he asked grumpily. 'It's the middle of the night!'

'It is us, Baera. It is me, Farença!'

'What do you want?'

'Open the door, Baera!' Mbemba said, almost yelling. 'Open up!'

The door eventually opened and the seer's silhouette filled the doorway. He yawned, polluting the night air with *nipa* fumes.

'Come in,' he said, 'I'll put a lamp on!'

He stumbled around trying to find the lamp and then struggled to light it. But eventually the glow lit up his face and they could tell by the colour of his eyes that he'd been drinking heavily. He was known for drinking the local firewater to excess and for spending most of what he earned from his consultations on it.

'Sit down and tell me what you want,' he said pointing to a mat. He plonked himself down at the opposite end.

'We want to know everything about Suplera and her

husband's trip,' said Mbemba, jumping in ahead of her mother, for she was now the more anxious of the two. 'We want to know everything that happened to them in Gorongoza, Kumalolo and Inhangoma!'

The fact that the seer was clearly inebriated did not bother them in the slightest. Everyone knew Baera got his inspiration from consuming *nipa*.

'Very well!' he said and stood up. He went over to a corner and came back with a dark green bag with red stripes. He sat back down and reached into the bag for his dice, which were also made from broken bits of turtle shell. He cupped his hands and threw the dice on the mat. He repeated the gesture several times, keeping up a monologue in which he evoked the souls of his dead ancestors: 'That there is Thomossene and that there is his wife. Yháá, Do you see, dear late Tchiposse? Do you see, dearly departed N'kuimba? Tell me everything!'

On he went, evoking different names, summoning his dead, until eventually he turned to his visitors and said: 'They all refuse! None of them will say anything!'

He spoke seriously now, as if he hadn't consumed a drop of alcohol. 'There's nothing more I can do,' he concluded.

'What? Try one more time!' pleaded Mbemba.

'No, there's no point. There's nothing I can do!' he said and he started to put the dice back in the bag. 'You might try another *n'tsango* or even a witch, but these things are being hidden.'

Mbemba looked at her mother but Farença said nothing. She didn't need to. Worry was written all over her face.

XVI

CAMPIRA IN SENA

Campira made his way back to Sena under clear skies, the sun's rays having flooded the land and its people from an early hour. He'd left Tchanaze, or Fineja, or whoever the woman was, with Phanga and he had a red cloth in his pouch containing bits he'd swept up from Phanga's floor, fragments of the dead that had come out of the woman's demonically possessed body. He was supposed to turn them into a potion to rub on Thomossene and Suplera, and he would do it too because he'd been ordered to do so by a man in league with the devil.

When the healer reached Sena, he made an effort to appear calm and inexpressive, to try not to betray the misgivings he felt in his heart. He went straight home but wasn't surprised to see that the four winds had spread news of his return and a crowd had formed at his door. He was surprised to see Nhamphandza and Baera among their number, for they were seasoned sears who ought to have been above village gossip and intrigue. Campira told them all to go home and get on with their lives, he was tired and would explain everything in due course. He went into his hut and heard the crowd mutter in protest outside, then gradually disperse.

A little later there was a knock at the door.

'Who is it?'

'It is me, Thomossene.'

'Go home and wait for me there,' Campira said without opening the door.'

'Understood,' said Thomossene.

Campira spent the rest of the day thinking about how best to proceed. He'd been told to bathe Thomossene and Suplera with the mysterious mixture and it was imperative that this be done away from prying eyes. Given the great interest the case had aroused, they would have to do it at night. But first he would make contact with the people that spoke to him from beyond the grave and instructed him in his art and craft. He would humbly ask for their guidance and wisdom during the bathing ceremony.

He put on his ceremonial robes and knelt down to invoke his ancestors. He summoned his dearly-departed grandfather and other dead relatives, wherever they lay, and begged them to hear his prayers. He kept this up until nightfall, for the secret to his success as a healer resided in his communicating with spirits who helped hm, though they spread chaos whenever they came to quench their thirst in the Zambeze's waters.

Later that night, Campira left his home and made his way to Thomossene and Suplera's house. As he walked he realised he would need the help of a ministrant, so he changed course and called upon the nearest one. It was late when he knocked and the household seemed to be asleep. He had to knock a second time before he heard any movement inside.

'Who is it?' asked a sleepy voice.

'Brumo, it is I!' said the healer, making sure to speak with purpose and vigour. This had the desired effect because the door promptly opened. 'Brumo, please get ready immediately!'

'Yes, master!' said Brumo. His voice was a little hesitant but he knew that if Campira came calling in the middle of the night it had to be for something urgent. He gathered his things and hurried back to the door.

'Tell your wife to get ready too!' said Campira, again speaking with authority.

'But master…!' Brumo stuttered.

'Do not argue,' the healer said. 'Call your wife. Come on, let's go!'

Brumo stared at him through tired, startled eyes. But he dared not protest and so he disappeared back into the hut, reappearing a minute later with Minória, his wife. She looked at the healer in drowsy bewilderment, but he just set off walking. He clearly wasn't about to explain things to her and when she turned to her husband, all he could do was shrug.

The night grew ever darker as Brumo and Minória followed Campira through the village. The healer was anxious for them not to cross paths with anyone who might recognise them, for they had to be discreet. Fortunately only the stars and the occasional night bird bore witness to their progress. No light from oil lamps or fireplaces escaped from the huts they passed and Campira was pleased that his ministrant did not break the silence by asking him what they were doing.

In fact Brumo could guess. He was aware of the rumours flying around, and as a ministrant, was privy to the healer's methods and movements. But Minória was as much in the dark as everyone else. She knew what the villagers had been saying about Tchanaze but Brumo never discussed professional matters at home. She'd always known that her husband was Campira's apprentice but it had never occurred to her that this might mean that she too would one day be called upon to intervene. In truth, Brumo was as surprised about this as she was. He couldn't imagine why his master had asked for Minória to accompany them, it had never happened before. No doubt the healer would have his reasons, but why tonight of all nights?

They eventually reached a hut that lay in total silence. Campira hammered on the door and a few seconds later a voice inside said: 'Who is it?'

'It is I, Campira,' replied the healer, and then they heard the sound of footsteps and the door opening. Thomossene stood there showing no sign of sleep or surprise, at least not until he saw that the healer had company. 'I've brought assistance,' was all Campira said.

'Come in,' said Thomossene, stepping aside and going over to light the oil lamp. The men's talking had alerted Suplera, though she hadn't been asleep either. She looked at Brumo and Minória with puzzlement too, but laid a mat out for everyone to sit down on.

'I know you are all eager to know what's happening but I cannot tell you anything for now,' said Campira. 'All I will say is that there is still a lot of work to be done and we must be patient and calm. I therefore ask the two women to light a fire, we will need plenty of hot water.'

He then gave them all a commanding stare, the kind that said he would say no more and did not expect to be asked to say more. The two women stood up and set about building a fire in the corner. Once the wood was set, Suplera fetched some oil and lit the thing. The men watched in silence, Thomossene desperate to know, but not daring to ask, what had happened after he and his wife had left Campira in Inhangoma standing before a burning hut.

'Now fill a pot with water, the largest pot in the house,' said Campira. 'Put it on the fire and let the water boil.'

The fire had got going now and the light of the flames licked their faces and brought warmth to the couple's humble abode. But humble though it may have been, it was still the place that had welcomed Tchanaze into the world, the fair maiden who had gone on to beguile every man from Sena to Chupanga.

They sat in silence waiting for the water to boil, nobody daring to initiate conversation. They were at the healer's beck and call and only he knew what the water was for.

'It's boiling!' Minória said, curiosity writ large across her face. 'It's ready!'

'Very good!' said Campira. 'Now take the pot out into the backyard. You can put the fire out too, we won't need it anymore.'

The two women carried the pot outside then came back in

and snuffed out the fire. They sat back down and looked at the healer expectantly. Without saying a word, he rose to his feet and went outside.

The night was cool and still, with no sense of foreboding despite what he was about to do. He took the red cloth from his pouch and sprinkled the human remains he'd brought from Kumalolo into the pot, then stirred them in with a stick. Steam rushed into the night air and the water gradually changed colour. It was impossible to tell what colour it had become and a funny smell, unlike anything his nostrils had ever encountered before, spread through the air. The stench was certainly not of this world and was so potent it had surely been prepared in the dungeons of hell. Campira went on stirring until the liquid cooled, whereupon he stuck his hand in. He took it out again and stirred some more, then went back to the door of the cabin and summoned Thomossene.

'Take your clothes off!' he instructed.

'What...?' said Thomossene.

'Take your clothes off, Thomossene!' Campira ordered, speaking more firmly this time.

So Thomossene stripped off under the stars and Campira proceeded to bathe him. Pieces of bone and other fragments of the unknown dead floated in the water, the foul smell of which did not escape Thomossene's attention. But he decided it was better not to know what the healer had done to the water and easier to just let him pour it over his body.

After a while, the healer decided the task was done and called for his assistant. When Brumo appeared, Campira handed him a strip of black fabric. 'Rub this man's body dry with this cloth!' he said.

Brumo was amazed by the sight that greeted him in the yard. But he said nothing, took the cloth and began to wipe Thomossene dry.

'Enough!' said the healer after a minute or two. 'Put your clothes on and go back inside.' Thomossene did as he was told and went back into the hut. Campira followed, and Brumo followed the healer.

'Now you, Suplera,' said the healer, 'go outside with Minória and she will bathe you and rub you dry with the cloth I've left there.'

The two women stood up hesitantly and went outside. The three men sat down on the mat and waited in silence for the women to return.

A few minutes later Minória reappeared at the door. 'I have done as you instructed,' she said, 'but there is still a lot of water left.'

'Very good, very good!' the healer said. 'Brumo, go and dig a hole and pour the remaining water into it. When it has fully soaked into the ground, take some of the wet soil from where we did the bathing and use it to cover the hole. Then come back in here.'

'Yes, master!' The ministrant stood up and took the hoe that was leaning against the wall. He went outside and the others soon heard him digging and scraping. They sat in silence thinking about everything that was happening, and about their lives and the spirits that hovered over Sena and its people. From somewhere in the village, the cry of a rooster announced the break of dawn.

'Master, I have finished,' said Brumo coming back into the hut and replacing the hoe against the wall. 'All done!'

'Excellent!' said the healer. 'You and your wife may go home now. Thank you for your work!'

Brumo and Minória stood up, nodded to the others and left. Brumo would have liked to have been told at least something about what they'd just been doing, although he knew his master would have his reasons for not sharing anything.

Thomossene, too, was eager for the healer to explain things. Now that they were alone, he turned to Campira in expectation, but the healer said nothing.

'How is our daughter?' said Thomossene, unable to contain himself. 'Did you find her?' His voice came out rather anxious and sad. He couldn't hide the fact that he and his wife believed the woman they'd met in Inhangoma was Tchanaze.

'She's in Kumalolo being treated by Phanga. He will get her back to her true self,' said the healer. His words brought Suplera comfort but also tipped her over the edge. She started to cry, her tears sparkling as they rolled down her cheek. They were the tears of a mother's despair, despair at the world and the power the spirits had over them.

'Stop crying, woman, the worst is over,' said Campira. 'You will soon have your daughter back, of this I can assure you. But first you must get ready because we will return to Kumalolo the day after tomorrow. Don't tell anybody, it must remain a secret, and don't tell anybody about your trip to Gorongoza or what happened in Inhangoma. Remember that your daughter is a victim of witchcraft and the perpetrators might live here in Sena!'

Thomossene met his wife's eyes. If the woman they'd seen in Inhangoma really was Tchanaze then of course, it had to be witchcraft. They'd not given this due consideration.

They'd accepted that their daughter's reappearance was the work of the spirits but they'd not given much thought to why she'd fallen ill in the first place, how she'd contracted *n'fúcua*. It was hard for them to imagine that anyone in Sena could have given it to her but the healer's words made them face up to the reality of their situation. They had to proceed with caution, for if the culprits did indeed live in Sena and were to learn of Tchanaze's recovery, they would surely do something to sabotage it.

'Don't forget, we set off for Kumalolo the day after tomorrow,' said Campira. 'I will come and get you myself.' Then he stood up, grabbed his pouch and headed out the door.

He made straight for home but, lost in his own thoughts, he failed to see two shadows sneak past him in the night. They belonged to two women whose hearts, like many hearts in Sena, burned with jealousy and the desire to cause neighbours harm.

Earlier that night, Mbemba had turned to Farença and said: 'I think we should go to Campira's house. He holds the key to this mystery and we cannot just sit here and wait, he might cast the *n'fúcua* back into me at any minute.'

Her voice sounded nervous and afraid but showed no sign of remorse. Her mother also feared the disease might be sent back into her daughter, a girl whose beads and braids no man had ever yearned for. The healer's return to Sena had made them both anxious and his silence only made matters worse.

'You are right, my child,' said Farença. 'We need to be vigilant and keep ourselves informed.'

They did not want people to see them creeping around and

so they waited for night to fall before they set off to Campira's house. The twinkle of stars in the sky was not enough to light up their faces but they stuck to the shadows anyway. Once the healer's hut was in sight, they ducked into the bush and found a spot from where they could watch his door. Light and smoke issued from cracks in the healer's hut's walls, but they hadn't been there long when the light went out and he appeared at the door. He shut it behind him, quickly and firmly, and set off down a nearby path. Mbemba and Farença followed. There were a number of cashew trees that they could hide behind if he turned around, but he didn't look over his shoulder once. He stopped outside Brumo's house.

'Why's he gone to see Brumo?' Mbemba whispered.

'Let's wait and see!' Farença replied.

They watched the healer knock on the door, saw the man of the house appear and then, a little while later, his wife. They knew Brumo was Campira's apprentice but what Minória had to do with anything they could not imagine. The couple left the house and set off with Campira into the night. Farença and Mbemba duly followed, wondering what it could all possibly mean. Eventually the healer led them to Tchanaze's parents' house.

'So that's where they were heading!' said Farença.

'You see, mother? I told you I had a funny feeling about this,' Mbemba sighed. 'We have to find out what they're up to.'

'You're right, my child!' said Farença. She steered her daughter into an orchard that offered a good view of the hut. They soon saw the flicker of flames through the walls and thick smoke rising into the starry sky. The backdoor opened and

Suplera and Minória carried a pot out into the yard. The fire in the hut went out and only the light of the oil lamp remained. Then Campira appeared in the backyard with Thomossene and proceeded to bathe him as if he were a child. This was too much for Farença and Mbemba, the strangeness of what they were seeing could only have one explanation: witchcraft. Mbemba began to shiver as if sensing the curse would soon be returned to her.

'Calm down my child,' her mother said, trying to reassure her, 'everything's going to be okay!'

But then they saw Minória bathe Suplera and then Brumo came out and started digging up the wet soil. They heard nothing of what was said but they saw everything and the whole horrible ritual terrified them.

Nevertheless, the terror they felt did not in any way translate to feelings of regret for the pain they'd caused to Tchanaze's parents. Mbemba would never repent of what she'd done, indeed she'd do it again tomorrow if necessary. She'd hated Tchanaze, the way she'd revelled in the menfolk's catcalls and whistles, but she'd also hated having *n'fúcua*, the way boys had crossed the street to avoid her and never paid her a compliment of any kind. Now she was free of the demonic disease, and despite her unremarkable looks, Sena's menfolk had finally started to notice her.

Brumo and Minória left the hut and Campira followed a few moments later.

'What should we do now, mother?' Mbemba asked.

'Let's follow Brumo and Minória!' said Farença.

The healer's apprentice and his wife had a head start and were inside their hut by the time Mbemba and Farença caught up with them. Farença knocked on the door.

'Who is it?' asked Brumo in a weary voice.

'It is me, Farença!' she said.

The door opened a fraction and Brumo looked out at them as if contemplating the devil.

'Huh?' he said. 'What on earth do you two want?'

'Calm down, Brumo, calm down,' said Farença nervously. 'We just want to talk to you, that's all.'

'Talk to me?' said Brumo. Then he turned to address his wife inside the hut. 'It's Farença and Mbemba. They want to talk to me!'

'Can we come in?' asked Mbemba, trying to sound nice.

'Oh, so now you want to come in as well?' he said, before stepping aside. 'Come on then.' The two women went in and they all sat down on a mat.

'What is it you want? It's way past our bedtime!' Brumo said uneasily. He was puzzled by their visit. Surely they knew he did not do consultations or cast spells, that he was still only a witch's apprentice.

'Look Brumo, we have something important to ask you,' said Farença, trying to sound calmer than she felt and struggling to decide how best to put it. 'We need you to be open with us.'

'Listen, Farença, it's late. Get to the point,' said Minória.

'Okay then, to begin with we want to know what you were doing at Thomossene's house?' said Farença, speaking without hesitation now. 'We know you both went there with Campira!'

Brumo and his wife looked at one another in amazement. 'How do you know we went there?' he asked.

'We saw you!' said Farença. 'As you know, the entire village is dying to know what's going on with this affair, and we're no different. We were coming back from visiting relatives, they'd held a *madzoca* séance, and when we passed Suplera's hut we saw you in the yard!'

Farença had lied shamelessly, desperate to get whatever information she could out of them.

But Brumo wasn't so easily fooled and he again exchanged looks with his wife. Their visitors were starting to make him nervous. Farença's vague words were not enough to explain why they were so keen to know about these things.

'Accepting that you saw us, so what? Why do you care?' he asked.

'No reason, no reason at all,' said Mbemba. 'We're just curious, like everyone else!'

'If you're so desperate to know what we were doing, go and ask Campira,' said Minória. 'He's the healer, not my husband!'

She was clearly losing patience and wanted them to leave.

'You were preparing some kind of spell to use against the people of Sena,' said Farença, 'that's why you had to do it at night. If word gets out, you'll be accused of witchcraft!' Her voice had been deliberately threatening to try and get Brumo on the defensive. It didn't work.

'I think you should leave now!' Brumo said. 'That's enough of that kind of talk, we want to go to bed.'

'I dare you to repeat what you just said to Campira!' Minória said, standing up and showing them the door. 'Now leave us alone!'

'Very well, come on my child!' said Farença. 'And repeat

to Campira my question about what evil you were cooking up is exactly what I'm going to do! Shame on you both!'

They stormed out, though they all knew Farença would do no such thing. The healer was too feared and respected to be asked questions like that.

'What now, mother?' asked Mbemba.

'Let's go and see N'tswairo,' said Farença. 'I know it's almost the morning but we cannot rest until we find out what's going on!'

The two shadows hastened through the early dawn in search of N'tswairo, a seer known for his ability to help those who'd suffered a misfortune. Farença and Mbemba had suffered many and now they needed him to prevent them from suffering another one.

N'tswairo lived with his six wives and twenty or so children in a compound that was close to Brumo's house. The seer provided for the whole clan through his craft, clients paying him either in money or a day's hard labour, for each of his wives farmed at least two plots.

When Farença and Mbemba entered the compound it was like they were in a village within the village. A dog barked but wagged its tail when it came over to investigate them. Otherwise everything was silent and still and this presented them with a major problem, for there was no way of knowing which hut N'tswairo would be in. He was known to sleep with a different wife every night and there was nothing to suggest he was in any hut in particular. Mbemba shrugged, went over to the nearest one and knocked. There was no answer so she tried again and eventually they heard movement inside.

'Who is it?' asked a sleepy female voice.

'We're looking for N'tswairo,' said Mbemba, 'we've come for a consultation!'

'Next one,' the sleepy voice replied.

They moved on to the next hut and knocked. This time Mbemba did not need to knock twice for they immediately heard someone come to the door.

'Who is it?' asked a male voice. They recognised it as the seer's and he sounded wide awake.

Farença took the lead this time: 'It is me, Farença, open the door, please, N'tswairo!'

The man opened the door with a puzzled look on his face. He was used to calls in the night but not at the break of dawn. Nevertheless, he welcomed them in and offered them a mat.

'What's the matter?' he asked.

'We need you to divine something for us,' Mbemba said and offered no further explanation. N'tswairo stood up and went into one of the other rooms, then returned with his *n'tsango* basket.

'So tell me, what do you want to know?' he said, getting his tortoise shell lots ready to cast.

'Everybody knows Suplera and her husband went to Gorongoza. We also know what happened when their daughter's grave was dug up, and there are rumours about a woman in Inhangoma. But that's all. There's a lot been left unsaid.'

'That is true, Farença,' said the seer.

'Well we want to know the rest!' said Mbemba jumping in. 'We want you to use your divination skills to tell us what we don't know!'

N'tswairo nodded and gathered in the lots. He held them

tightly in his hands and then tossed them on the mat.

'Right, let's see! Look, here they are in Gorongoza. That's Inhangoma and that's Kumalolo, do you see? Oh, there they are, there they are!' He continued with his broken monologue for a while, but then stopped and turned to them.

'No, I can't find anything!' he said.

'Please try again!'

'Okay, Mbemba, I'll try.' He gathered in his lots and threw them again but he didn't seem to be getting anywhere. He stood up and went into the bedroom. When he reappeared he was wearing a red cloth with black stripes. He sat back down and started all over again, then stopped and stared at them. His face had become a deep frown.

'What?' said the two women in unison, alarmed by the seer's expression.

'I still cannot see anything, Farença,' replied N'tswairo. But noting the disappointed looks on their faces, he cast the lots again. He sighed. 'You see those two lots? They mean death. So I can see two deaths, but that's it.'

His words cut through them like a knife.

'Two deaths?' Mbemba asked in a shaky voice. 'Whose deaths?'

'Two deaths. That's all I can see,' said N'tswairo.

'But whose deaths? Who's going to die, N'tswairo?' Mbemba insisted.

'Look, child, the answers are hidden. I cannot uncover anything else,' said the seer. He'd seen the effect his divination had had on them and started to pack his things away. 'That's it, sorry!'

Mother and daughter made their way back home as dawn

broke. They'd wanted to know more, of course, but N'tswairo had made it clear that further questions would be futile. It was worrying enough that he'd been able to divine so little, but that he'd seen two deaths was chilling.

'Now what?' Mbemba asked.

'My child, we have to go back to Kumalolo and see Mabureza as soon as possible,' said Farença. 'He started this, after all.'

'Yes, mother, you're right,' said Mbemba. She agreed, of course, but the prospect of seeing Mabureza again daunted her. He was not someone you wanted to get close to too often.

They hurried home to avoid being seen by anyone. A few more hours and the faces of adults and children would appear at windows and in doorways ready to embrace the new day. The sight of the sun rising up over Sena filled some people with love for their land, while for others it brought sadness that such a beautiful place should be in thrall to the madness of ghosts.

Once the sun was properly up, Brumo went straight to his master's house. The events of the previous night had been most unusual and he thought he ought to inform Campira of Farença and Mbemba's visit. He'd assisted Campira enough times over the years to know that it was unlikely the two women had seen them performing a ritual in someone's backyard by chance. It was likewise hard to believe that casual curiosity had brought them knocking on his door in the middle of the night. He thought the healer should know and his wife agreed.

'You should go over to Campira's house right now and tell him everything,' she said. 'Those two little she-devils spying on us like that, it's outrageous!'

Brumo bumped into several people on the way but he found the healer's house enveloped in silence. Campira lived on his own, for his wife and children had moved out to Inhangoma where he planned to join them one day, when one of his apprentices was ready to take over. Brumo was one such apprentice, of course, and he knew his master did not like to be disturbed until late morning. Mornings were sacred for witches, a time for communing with the spirits that guided them in their craft. So rather than knock, Brumo sat down and waited. He greeted passersby and watched the sun climb ever higher, until finally he heard movement inside the hut. He stood up and knocked.

'Who is it?' said the healer. His voice wasn't very welcoming and suggested he wasn't prepared to open the door to just anyone.

'It is me, Brumo!'

'So early?'

'Yes, master, I bring important news!'

'Very well,' said the healer.

Campira opened the door wearing the *capulanas* he favoured of a morning. He stepped aside and let his ministrant in.

'Master, listen!' said Brumo, and he proceeded to give a brief but detailed account of Farença and Mbemba's visit.

'Interesting! Very interesting indeed!' said Campira. Then almost to himself he added: 'Why are they so concerned about this? Can it be simple curiosity or is there more to it than that?'

'In my opinion, master, they are hiding something,' said Brumo. 'Why else would they be watching you?'

'You're right, no one in Sena would ordinarily dare follow me,' said the healer. 'They have some explaining to do!'

Campira disappeared into his bedroom. When he reappeared, he was fully clothed.

'Let's go and find them!' he said. 'But first we should warn Thomossene and his wife.'

They set off, pausing to greet whoever they met on the way, people who dared not ask Campira about Tchanaze, though it was the main topic of conversation in the village. They found Thomossene and Suplera sitting on a mat on their verandah.

'We're not setting off yet, are we?' asked Thomossene, standing up to greet them.

'No,' said Campira. 'Let's go inside, I've something to tell you.'

They went in and sat down and Campira quickly presented them with the facts.

'Now that is odd!' said Thomossene.

'Very strange,' said Suplera rather crossly. 'Who do they think they are, spying on us?'

'Let's go and find out!' said the healer.

They set off walking through the village bound for Farença and Mbemba's house. People stopped and stared as they passed, but it was a short walk and they soon reached the women's hut. Campira listened for a moment and then knocked. There was no answer. He tried again but there was obviously nobody home.

'Where could they have gone?' Brumo wondered out loud.

'I'll go and ask a neighbour,' said Campira, and he set off

for the next hut.

He came back a few minutes later wearing a puzzled look.

'What?' asked Suplera.

'They left first thing this morning without saying where they were going,' said Campira. 'This is all very strange!'

'Indeed it is, master.'

'But there's nothing else we can do for now,' the healer said. 'Brumo, you should go home, and Thomossene, you and your wife should do likewise. I'll call for you later.'

They walked along together for a while before heading off in their respective directions. Campira's mind was a whirr. What was going on? What were the two women up to? He could find no satisfactory answers to these and other questions, but one thing was for certain: something strange was afoot and neither Phanga nor the spirits had warned him about it.

XVII

FARENÇA AND MBEMBA IN KUMALOLO

Though Farença and Mbemba hadn't slept all night, they decided to set off for Kumalolo immediately. N'tswairo's divination of two deaths had left them shaken and the strange ritual they'd witnessed in Suplera and Thomossene's yard, coupled with the rumours of Tchanaze's reincarnation, were more than enough to warrant going to see Mabureza.

Besides, they knew that as soon as day broke, Brumo would run to Campira's house and inform him of their late-night visit. Campira was only a healer, no match for a great witch like Mabureza, but he still practised witchcraft and he was highly respected and feared in Sena, he wasn't someone you wanted to get on the wrong side of. It seemed wise to make themselves scarce.

They walked all through the day, climbing hills and descending valleys, desperate to get to Kumalolo as soon as possible. But their lack of sleep eventually caught up with them and they realised they'd have to stop and rest somewhere. They had relatives in Tchangadeia, a village on the other side of Caia, towards Kuamarra, and so, with the sun fast disappearing over the horizon, Farença led them there.

Night had fallen by the time they knocked on the door but they were given an enthusiastic welcome, for the home belonged to Muti, Farença's brother-in-law, Mbemba's paternal uncle, and they'd not visited him for several years. Muti lived with his wife and nine children and worked as a rafter on the Zangue river, a tributary of the Zambeze, transporting vehicles from one side to the other.

After the customary greetings, he asked them where they were going and whether he could help them with anything.

'No, we don't need anything, thanks,' said Farença. 'We're just on our way to Kumalolo.'

'Kumalolo?' asked Muti, startled, for he knew very well why people went there. 'You're going to Kumalolo?'

'That's what I said,' Farença replied, trying to be genial.

'But why? What kind of trouble takes you there?' asked Muti.

'Well, as you know, your niece suffers from *n'fúcua,'* said Farença. 'We heard someone moved there recently who's capable of curing the disease.'

'Ah, I understand,' said Muti. 'But Kumalolo is a dangerous place, you should be accompanied by a man. I'll go with you.'

'No!' said Farença. 'There's really no need, we don't want to bother you.'

'It's no bother at all, I'll go with you. As you know, there are some very strange individuals who live there.'

'We'll be fine just the two of us!' Farença said, friendly but firm. 'We'd really rather be on our own and not have you worrying about us.'

Muti was quiet for a while as he thought things through, but he nodded and didn't bring the matter up again. They talked some more and settled down for the night. In the early hours, they rose again, bid Muti farewell and promised to stop by on their way back.

The two women resumed their journey in silence, fortified from having had a proper rest. Their resolve had strengthened too and they couldn't wait to see Mabureza and hear what he had to say. They needed to know what N'tswairo couldn't see and whose deaths he'd divined, and they needed to know whether anyone had found out that they were responsible for Tchanaze's death.

When they finally got to Kumalolo, it looked the same as it always did. They crossed paths with the usual people, passed the usual houses, encountered the usual vegetation. The breeze that blew in off the Zambeze was even the same as usual, bringing the fresh smell of reeds and the less fresh smell of mildew. Bright coloured birds danced and chirped on either side of the path, as on previous visits. The two women even felt the same mixture of sensations that they always felt upon entering Kumalolo: fear, on the one hand, for it was a place steeped in black magic; hope on the other, for it had answers to every problem. Farença and Mbemba were not alone in this and the air was thick with the hopes and fears of others, for everyone who made the pilgrimage to Kumalolo did so with the intention of harnessing the powers of its witches for great ill or great gain.

Farença and Mbemba made their way purposefully towards the cabin where Mabureza lived. Their approach sent the occasional bird flapping out from the reeds and flying off down the river, but the hut itself, set a little way back from the river, stood quiet and still. Unlike last time, Mabureza did not appear at the door as they approached. They went up and knocked, waited and tried again, and then again. When no one answered for a fourth time, they looked at one another concerned. They didn't know Mabureza very well, of course, but witches didn't tend to go anywhere. As a rule, they had no friends or relatives or acquaintances, at least not living ones, so they didn't tend to socialise, and it was hard to imagine someone as horrible as Mabureza becoming romantically involved with anyone.

They looked around for signs of life but realised, with growing disquiet, that the place seemed not to have been occupied for some time. The yard was overgrown with sedge, and peering through a window, there was even sedge growing inside. The cabin looked utterly uninhabited. Alarm now spread through them as they were confronted by the facts: Mabureza no longer lived here.

'He obviously doesn't live here anymore,' said Mbemba. 'Now what are we going to do?'

'You're right, this house has been abandoned,' said Farença, trying, but failing to hide the worry in her voice. Because if they couldn't find Mabureza, if he'd disappeared, they really were in trouble.

'He cannot have just vanished, someone must know where he went,' said Mbemba. 'Come on, we'll ask the neighbours.' This sounded tenacious but that wasn't how she felt, for she too knew that they were lost without Mabureza.

The two women therefore set off walking along the riverbank somewhat shaken. They hadn't gone far when they came upon a cabin, and before they'd even had a chance to think about knocking, a female figure appeared in the doorway. She had a physique unlike anything they'd ever seen, for she was very, very thin and bare chested, but with breasts so shrivelled and droopy they could hardly be seen under all her beads and tattoos. She was clearly one of Kumalolo's legions of witches and had likely never owned the body she was now in. Farença and Mbemba were too intimidated to know what to say.

'My daughters,' the woman said, looking them over with a sinister smile, 'how can I help you?'

Her voice sounded like thunder and was neither that of a woman nor a man. Farença and Mbemba stood there frozen, convinced that they'd come upon the devil in female form.

'I said how can I help you?' the woman repeated, evidently sensing their helplessness. 'You look lost. Are you perhaps looking for someone?'

'Yes, lady, we are looking for a man named Mabureza,' said Farença, forcing herself to be brave but speaking in a weak and trembling voice. 'He used to live over there but he seems to have moved.'

'Never heard of him!' the woman said, and she turned around and slammed the door in their faces.

Farença and Mbemba turned around too and ran. They could not get away from the woman fast enough and hoped never to lay eyes on her again.

Running, they soon came upon another cabin where a man was pottering about in his yard. He stopped what he was doing and raised a hand in greeting. He looked like a normal person, in other words he didn't seem to be any kind of witch, warlock, healer or seer, for not everyone in Kumalolo was involved in witchcraft. Some people led quite ordinary lives, or as ordinary as was possible in a place where spirits had been living in the bodies of others for generations.

'What brings you to these parts?' he said and his smile almost made them cry with relief.

'We came to see someone,' said Farença, catching her breath and smiling back. 'But he wasn't in his cabin, and judging by the state of the place, he seems to have moved. He's called Mabureza.'

The man's expression changed at mention of the witch's name.

'Ah, yes, I know who you mean, he was pretty well known around here,' the man said. 'But he left town some time ago.'

'You mean he no longer lives in Kumalolo?' asked Mbemba.

'That's right,' said the man, more wary of them now. 'He just seemed to disappear.'

'Well he must have gone somewhere,' said Mbema, a bit snappier than she'd intended. 'Does no one know where he went?'

'Someone said he went to Morrumbala, but I don't know.'

'Morrumbala? That's on the other side of the river, isn't it?' said Farença. 'Are you sure? Because we'll go there if you are. We really need to find him.'

'I'm not sure, no. But it's easy enough to try, you can get a canoe to Morrumbala from just down there. Ask around, if he's moved there, people will know, he's hard to ignore!'

'Thanks,' said Farença, 'we'll do that.'

'Who's the woman in the cane hut?' asked Mbemba, still shaken by their earlier encounter.

'Oh, she's called Nhahana apparently,' said the man. 'Nobody knows much about her, she just suddenly appeared, around the same time Mabureza left in fact. I guess she's another witch—just what Kumalolo needs!'

The man laughed but Mbemba shuddered. The woman was undoubtedly a witch and it was no surprise that no one knew anything about her.

They took a canoe across the river and were feeling positive again by the time they'd reached the other side. If Mabureza was in Morrumbala they'd soon find him and all their worries would be over.

Morrumbala looked a lot like Sena in that it was a sparsely populated sprawl of solitary cabins, compounds and little clusters of huts. The sun was setting and people were gathering around fires having returned from their daily chores. Farença and Mbemba stopped at the first house they came to where a group of people were sitting outside.

'You don't look like you're from round here!' said a big burly man, apparently the head of the household.

'No, we're from Sena,' said Farença. 'This is our first

time in Morrumbala.'

The man gestured for them to sit down on a mat.

'And what brings you here?'

'We're looking for a man who moved here from Kumalolo a few months ago,' said Farença.

Their host looked them over with increased curiosity.

'From Kumalolo, huh? What's his name?'

'He's called Mabureza and we really need to find him!' Mbemba cut in.

The man flinched. Either he hadn't been expecting Mbemba to speak or the name meant something to him. He looked the two women up and down again.

'Well I'll be damned,' he said. 'I hear he's a man like no other.'

They waited for him to say more but he didn't. He'd turned rueful, perhaps unwilling to involve himself in matters of this kind.

'Do you know where we can find him?' said Farença, choosing to ignore the man's signals.

'I've no idea. I didn't even know he'd moved here until you just said it!' Then he appeared to take pity on them and added: 'You might try N'khambala, he lived in Kumalolo for a number of years. If anyone knows, he will. His cabin's just up ahead.'

The two women thanked the man and bid the family farewell. They walked on for a few minutes and then came to the next house. Like the previous one, it was made of bamboo poles daubed with red clay. Thick smoke escaped from one of the windows, though there didn't seem to be anyone around.

Night had now drawn in, though the moon was yet to

rise, giving the stars a chance to sparkle. The two women approached the house, and seeing that the door was ajar, called out 'Hello' rather than knock. A man appeared, quite old, with a very still presence. The light from inside the hut lit up their faces as he opened the door.

'We're looking for N'khambala,' said Farença.

'I am N'khambala!' he said in a voice that was very hesitant, as if making himself audible was a struggle. But his gaze was firm. He seemed to be trying to work out if he'd seen them somewhere before.

'It's just that we need to find Mabureza, a man who used to live in Kumalolo. We heard he'd moved here and someone said you might know where to find him,' Farença explained. The man's expression changed. He seemed to know who Mabureza was and be impressed that the two women should be looking for him.

But then he said: 'Nobody of that name lives here in Morrumbala!'

Farença and Mbema both slumped. 'Are you sure?' said Farença.

'Look, I used to live in Kumalolo and I know the fellow you mean,' said N'khambala. 'And I can promise you, he's not here in Morrumbala.'

'Well if he's not here then where the hell is he?' said Mbemba.

N'khambala smiled, perhaps amused at her choice of phrase. 'If you really want to know, you'd best come in.'

The old man ushered them through the door and gestured for them to sit down on a mat. There was a fireplace in one corner, the source of the smoke they'd seen escaping from the window, and ornamental objects hung on the walls, including terrapin and turtle shells. N'khambala was evidently a witch or a seer. Now they understood why he'd lived in Kumalolo and why he'd invited them in.

He noticed them looking. 'The spirits will know where to find him,' he said and he went over to a large chest by the fireplace and took out his witch's mask. He put this on and then added other items from the chest, strange things that he either hung around his neck or draped over his shoulders. Chief among them was a necklace of shells and beads that shone, not in the light of the fire, but of their own accord. He then began to sing a hymn while beating his hands against his chest, inviting wandering souls to leave their tombs and lead him to Mabureza.

The hymn ended with a roar, and then another one, and then N'khambala started slapping himself, quite hard. He'd been transformed, from elderly and weak to powerful and mighty. Then he suddenly sat down and fell silent. The only sound in the room became the crackle of the fire. Then just as suddenly, he stood up and took his mask off, followed by his other adornments, and put them back in the chest. With everything tidied away, he became the dear old man who'd invited them in again. He sat back down and looked at them, smiling.

'What's going on?' said Farença.

'Nothing!' said N'khambala. 'I consulted my ancestors, that's all.'

Farença and Mbemba exchanged confused looks.

'And?' asked Farença. 'What did they say?'

'Well, Mabureza certainly isn't in Morrumbala,' said

N'khambala. 'Or Kumalolo for that matter.'

'So where is he then?' said Mbemba, becoming impatient.

'He doesn't seem to be anywhere!'

The two women were becoming exasperated. 'But we don't understand!' said Farença.

'Then I will try to be clearer,' said N'khambal. 'Mabureza had been inhabiting a skeleton that previously belonged to a man named Nhambire, who drowned with two friends in the Zambeze. The body he had when you met him did not belong to him.'

'His body did not belong to him? What do you mean?' asked Farença, though she was beginning to understand. She knew witches in Kumalolo were said to inhabit bodies that were not their own.

'It is not really for me to explain,' said N'khambala. 'But basically the man the skeleton belonged to decided that Mabureza must abandon it, due to some sort of conflict between the two of them, I don't know the details. So one day Mabureza left Kumalolo and he told people he was coming here. But he never did come. What he actually did was jump back in the river. Now do you understand?'

They thought they did, or at least some of it. If he'd jumped into the river and vanished, or gone back to the underworld or wherever, that did at least explain why nobody seemed to know where he was. But it did nothing to help their situation. N'tswairo had foreseen two deaths. Theirs? Who had revealed this to him? Who could they turn to for protection if Mabureza had abandoned them? Their heads filled with these and other questions, all of them impossible to answer, all of them pointing to a single other question: what should they do now?

'What should we do now?' said Farença.

'Do not lose heart!' said N'khambala. 'Go back to Kumalolo and find a woman who recently settled there. According to my ancestors, she should be able to help you.'

Farença and Mbemba's expressions changed. They desperately needed some form of hope to cling on to.

'What's her name?' said Farença.

'Nhahana,' said N'khambala, and the two women shuddered. Their encounter with the old lady was still raw in the memory. They shook their heads and cursed their fates, the last thing either of them wanted was to come face to face with her again.

'She'll be glad to help you, I'm sure,' N'khambala said cheerily and they made an effort to look grateful. After all, they had been fortunate to meet the man sitting before them and they thanked him profusely before leaving. He invited them to sleep the night in his cabin but they politely declined. It was common knowledge that anyone visiting Morrumbala should refuse such offers. People in Morrumbala had a reputation for using spells in the night to suck out the energy of sleeping guests, which they then used to perform their agricultural tasks the following day.

Thus Farença and Mbemba refused the invitation even though night had firmly set in. A golden disc of a moon shone down over the village's thatched roofs as the two women set off walking without knowing where they were heading. It was too late to get a canoe back to Kumalolo, the boatmen would have all taken to their beds.

'Where will we spend the night, mother?'

Farença thought for a moment then said: 'Let's try the

council chamber.'

Travellers obliged to spend nights in unfamiliar places often chose to bed down among the sick at the local health centre. But Morrumbala didn't have a health centre so mother and daughter made their way to the council chamber instead. They found it closed, silent and dark. Undeterred, they went around the back, for that was generally where the guard's outhouse was. Sure enough they found the guard sitting beside a campfire with his wife. They were chatting away animatedly but stopped abruptly when they noticed the presence of strangers. The guard stood up and approached them in a hostile fashion.

'Good evening!' said Farença.

'Good evening. What do you want?' said the guard.

'We need somewhere to spend the night,' Farença said. 'We've missed the last boat to Kumalolo.'

'Kumalolo!' The man stiffened. 'What business have you there?'

'Oh, nothing,' Farença said, playing it cool. 'We're from Sena. We've been visiting relatives in Mopeia and Kumalolo is the nearest crossing.'

She'd chosen her words carefully and it worked. The man looked relieved and dropped his aggressive act. He went over to his wife and talked to her for a moment, then came back.

'You may spend the night here with us,' he said and he led them over to the fire and pointed for them to sit down. This they did and the guard's wife offered them food. They ate and chatted about mundane things until the moon left the sky and they fell asleep under the twinkling stars.

They rose early the next morning, thanked their hosts and

set off for the river. There were already one or two boatmen ready to cross and they took a canoe back to Kumalolo, Morrumbula having made a favourable impression. Its people had been friendly and helpful, not least N'khambala, a man who, like most witches, preferred to lead a life of solitude.

But now a different witch interested them: Nhahana. She would put them in touch with Mabureza, who had mysteriously thrown himself into the Zambeze. Or thrown the body he was inhabiting into the river, or the body had thrown him in, it wasn't very clear. Either way, he'd disappeared into the murky waters of the river and they contemplated those murky waters now as fish and crocodiles came to the surface, lured by the sun's first rays.

There was no sign of Nhahana at the cabin where they'd first met her. One or two birds flew around the yard, breaking the morning silence with their chirruping, but no one came to the door to greet them.

'Should we knock?' said Mbemba tentatively. Farença hesitated too, for she was as wary of the old lady as her daughter.

'Let's wait a bit first,' she decided.

They moved away from the door and stood under a tree. They felt awkward lingering there, waiting for a woman to appear who hadn't invited them to come and who they didn't really want to see. But they had no choice, she was their only hope. The threat of two deaths hung over them for a start, but they were also eager to see Mabureza for there were so many things that needed explaining. Nobody in Sena knew what had happened in Inhangoma or Gorongoza and it was being hidden from the seers. Tchanaze was supposed to be alive when they had witnessed her death with their own eyes. And now there was Mabureza's own disappearance and his feigned or aborted move to Morrumbula.

They waited for a long time and started to think the hut must be empty. But then they heard a deep voice chanting, a song they knew witches used to summon the dead, followed by a gruff voice striking up a conversation with someone who either wasn't there or didn't answer. The dialogue-monologue came to an end with a howl so piercing it made Farença and Mbemba jump. It was unlike the howl of any animal they knew and indeed it was so loud and strange they found it hard to believe it had come from inside the hut. Then the cabin itself began to shake. Something was slamming into the walls and they knew it had to be the witch hurling herself around the room. Then they heard her writhing on the floor, thrashing around in a mixture of pleasure and pain, culminating in a moment of ecstasy, then silence.

Suddenly the door opened and Nhahana appeared in the doorway, shaking and screaming. At first the two women thought she was angry with them, but then she started running around the outside of the cabin, round and round demonically in laps. Her droopy breasts flailed about as she circled the hut and blood poured from her mouth and nose, splattering over her beads and a necklace made of human fingers and teeth. Mbemba was seized by a feeling of great pity and fear and she clung to her mother like a child. But Farença was just as terrified and they held each other tight, for neither of them had seen anything so gruesome before.

Nhahana didn't so much as glance in their direction, she just carried on running and screaming, indifferent to everything around her. Several minutes passed in this way, then she went back into the cabin and shut the door. The screaming continued inside, interspersed with howls of the kind a rabid dog might make that was angry, starved and about to turn on its owner. Then the walls began to shudder again. Nhahana was a frail old lady but she hurled her body around with merciless force, pounding herself into the walls until a thud indicated that she'd fallen to the floor. There was yet more thrashing around, and then silence. Not a sound emerged from the cabin for quite some time but Mbemba and Farença kept on waiting, staring at the door, expecting it to open at any moment. It didn't.

The sun nudged up to the top of the sky and sent its rays down hard and heavy. There was not a cloud in sight and even the breeze off the river blew warm. One or two birds traced occasional circles in the air but otherwise the hours passed by without incident. Then finally the door opened. Nhahana appeared at the threshold, her already disfigured body all the worse for being splattered with blood, now dried and congealed. She stared at them with no hint of a smile, a stupid expression on her face as if she were quite mad, as if she had in fact just escaped from a lifetime's internment at a lunatic's asylum. But she raised a hand and beckoned for them to come closer. Then she ushered them into the cabin and pointed to a mat on the floor, taking a three-legged stool for herself.

'What do you want?'

Her voice had the same unfriendly tone as before and that same strange pitch that was neither male nor female. It struck fear into Farença and Mbemba, just as it had done the first time, though there was something strangely familiar about it too.

'I said what do you want? Why are you bothering me?'

Mother and daughter exchanged looks and Farença realised she'd have to take the lead.

'We're looking for Mabureza!' she said.

'Who's he?'

'He used to live over there.'

'What's it got to do with me?'

'Well, we went to Morrumbala,' said Farença, making a big effort to be brave and stand up to this woman, or whoever it was she was talking to. 'A man there named N'khambala said you'd be able to help us find Mabureza.'

Nhahana scowled but remained silent. Then she stood up and went over to a basket that was hanging on the wall and took out a piece of bone. What animal the bone had once belonged to it was impossible to say, but the witch held it up to her nostrils and sniffed at it.

'Oh, Mabureza! Why didn't you say so?' she snarled before sniffing again. 'That man no longer lives here. The owner of the body he was inhabiting needed it back.'

She stopped sniffing for a moment and looked at her guests, as if inviting them to comment on what she'd just said.

'Yes, that's what N'khambala told us,' said Farença. 'But where did he go? What happened to him?'

'He jumped in the river,' the witch said, sniffing the bone again. 'You're upset about the *n'fúcua* he transferred into Tchanaze, I suppose?'

'That's it!' Mbemba blurted out, encouraged by the woman's powers of divination. But rather than say anything else, the witch stood up and put the mysterious bone back in its basket.

'Well, there's nothing to worry about,' she said. 'While you were outside, I consulted my people, Mabureza included. I visited him where his spirit reposes and he told me to tell you not to worry. He'll find another body to use and come back in a few days' time and solve your problem. Understood?'

She stared down at them enigmatically from her stool, her expression unreadable.

'Yes, we understand,' said Farença, feeling cautiously cheered. 'But what should we do? We're worried about two deaths that a seer in Sena saw and we're worried the local healer might find out it was us who asked Mabureza to kill Tchanaze.'

'Firstly, don't mention Mabureza's name to anyone in Sena, understood? Good, because you must know that Mabureza will never abandon you. So don't worry about what some seer said. Go back to Sena and come back here in three days, Mabureza will be waiting for you. Take heed for I have spoken!'

XVIII

CAMPIRA, THOMOSSENE AND SUPLERA IN KUMALOLO

Campira, Thomossene and Suplera made their way to Kumalolo having set off earlier than planned. The events of the previous night, specifically the actions of Mbemba and her mother, had precipitated their departure and continued to trouble the healer. The bathing ritual should not have been witnessed by outside eyes, this went against the conventions of their profession and Campira would have to inform Phanga. Then there was the question of why it had been witnessed and where Mbemba and Farença had gone before sunrise.

Thoughts of Tchanaze also troubled the healer. He had taken her to Kumalolo from Inhangoma and left her there, dazed, in the care of a man clearly in league with the devil. What sort of state would she be in when they got there? Would she still think she was Fineja or would she have gone back to being her true self? Because as far as Campira was concerned, the two women were one and the same.

Assuming Phanga had worked his magic and she'd gone back to being Tchanaze, how would her parents react? What about Sena's menfolk? For years, they'd been infatuated by her beauty, only to then lose her. How would they respond to her coming back from the dead? Deferentially or in a frenzy of lustful hysteria?

He also thought about how he would feel himself once word of her resurrection spread. As the healer who'd made it happen, he'd be acclaimed from Sena to Inhangoma to Kumalolo, from Save to Matchaze and even the lands of the Machopes and the Macuas, and the acclaim would rub off on his apprentices too, who deserved it, for they'd assisted in two burial ceremonies for a start. Phanga, meanwhile, would be hailed as some kind of supreme witch and an exotic specimen at that. People would travel for days and even weeks to see him, and who knew what kind of wanton sorcery that might lead to?

Which brought him back to Farença and Mbemba. Campira sincerely hoped they had nothing to do with any of this because if they had, Phanga would surely bring all hell crashing down on them.

'Let's stop here!' Campira said, pointing to a tree by the side of the road. Thomossene and Suplera came to a halt, a little startled by his impromptu command, for they too had been lost in thought.

The three travellers sat down in the shadow of the tree. Campira cleared his throat and looked the couple firmly in the eyes before speaking. 'Now listen carefully to what I have to say: Fineja, or rather Tchanaze, your daughter, is in Kumalolo with Phanga. He's been giving her a series of treatments because what happened to her has scrambled her mind to the point that she does not recognise herself. I took her to him from Inhangoma and he gave me the mixture you bathed with in Sena. I was carrying out the warlock's instructions only, as you know, we were seen by intruders and…'

'Is Tchanaze okay?' Suplera cut in, understandably anxious to find out more about her daughter. 'Did she ask after us?'

'She's fine, woman, relax, but please, no interrupting!' said Campira. 'What I mean to say is that in Kumalolo we will probably have to repeat the bathing ritual, for let me be clear, we must carry out Phanga's instructions to the letter.'

'When will we be able to take our daughter home?' said Thomossene. Like his wife, he seemed incapable of containing himself any longer.

'That is none of your business!' Campira said sharply, and he gave them both a firm stare. 'Phanga will tell us what to do and when to do it. If he wishes you to know something, you will know it. Otherwise, try not to think about it and definitely do not ask. Understood?'

'Yes,' they both said, nodding.

'In that case, let's get back on the road!'

They walked through the night without stopping again to

rest, such was their eagerness to get to where they were going. Dawn broke as they began the final stretch and they reached Kumalolo at sunrise, with a cool breeze blowing in off the river. The atmosphere was nevertheless heavy because the air in Kumalolo was always thick with witchcraft. It was a place that drew people with problems to solve, illnesses to cure, disappointments to overcome, love that remained stubbornly unrequited. People came seeking a spell to attract a lover or a river herb to make them irresistible to a neighbour's husband or wife. Others came craving a windfall, quick and easy money perhaps, or a bumper harvest, or something to make sure their fishing nets attracted more catfish than anyone else's.

The first sunrays of the day hit the warlock's hut just as Campira, Thomossene and Suplera approached it. The place was utterly lifeless, there weren't even any birds chirping, the silence was deafening. They sat down on a log in the yard, exhausted from walking all night, and readied themselves to wait. It was the time of day when witches made contact with their friends in the underworld and communed with the previous owners of the bodies they possessed. Sure enough, noises soon emerged from inside the hut, something like the roar of a wild beast followed by the howl of a hunger-stricken wolf. Then came the sound of Phanga banging into the walls and a crescendo of screaming until the hut itself began to shake. From where they were sitting, it sounded like absolute pandemonium had broken out inside the hut and even Campira was left dumbfounded. He was a witch himself but there were major differences. Campira was a witch and a man, in other words he was alive and had yet to die. Phanga, on the other hand, was a witch and a ghost: he'd died and gone to hell, escaped and come to practice witchcraft on earth by inhabiting the body of another.

The tumult in the hut eventually died down and was replaced by heavy breathing. Birds began to dart across the sky and their melody lifted the mood of the anxious visitors. Then the door swung open and a bony, skeletal figure appeared at the threshold, blood dripping from his mouth, his face full of cuts and bruises. He beckoned them in and pointed to a bale of reeds for them to sit on. As their eyes adjusted to the light they realised he was alone. Thommosene and Suplera looked uneasily at Campira, wondering where their daughter was, and the healer in turn looked at the warlock.

'Don't look at me like that!' barked Phanga. 'Tchanaze is with N'tchimica, I sent her away for further treatment. You will see her soon!'

What he'd said was evidently supposed to reassure them but his voice, so rough and harsh, made them feel even more unsettled.

'Campira, my friend, tell me how you have been and what you have managed to achieve!' said Phanga, and again, although his words were civil, he delivered them like a slap in the face.

'We travelled well!' said Campira, more composed than the others. 'I did everything just as the great master instructed, but something unforeseen and untoward happened.' He went on to explain about being seen by Mbemba and Farença.

'Who is this Mbemba person?' asked the warlock. This new development clearly had his full attention.

'Mbemba is a girl from Sena,' said the healer. 'She has suffered from *n'fúcua* since she was a child, although lately she appears to have healed somewhat. I don't know what their interest is in all this.'

'You don't know what their interest is? My dear Campira, you soon will!' said Phanga. 'How dare they interfere with my work?'

He fell silent for a moment and appeared to be deep in thought.

'Fine, we'll repeat the treatment right here,' he finally said. 'But let me assure you, I have not finished with them!'

Campira nodded. 'We await your instructions, great master!'

'Very well then, you, woman, take this pot of water and make a fire with lots of wood, bring it to the boil!'

Suplera stood up and did as Phanga had ordered. There was a small fireplace in the corner and she filled it with wood and placed the pot over it. After a few minutes, she had flames crackling and a cloud of smoke spiralled out of the window.

In the meantime, Phanga got his basket and took out an assortment of potions only he knew the origins of. He began to prepare a mixture that seemed like the one Campira had taken to Sena. The healer got a better look at it this time: there were bits of aquatic plants and tubers uprooted from the bowels of the Zambeze, along with fragments of human body parts, no doubt sourced from the same place.

'The water is boiling, master!' Suplera said.

'Well done!' replied the warlock, wiping a drip of blood from his mouth with the back of his hand. He went over to the pot, saw that she'd used plenty of wood and confirmed that the water was bubbling sufficiently. Then he poured a large amount of his concoction into the pot and stirred it in with a stick. A strange, nauseating smell rose into the air, a smell that gave no indication of what was brewing. Phanga stuck to his task for several minutes and the smell became increasingly foul until the visitors from Sena found it hard to believe what their own noses were detecting. But then Phanga abruptly stopped, poured some of the liquid onto the wood to put the fire out and sat down opposite them again.

'We must wait for the medicine to cool,' he said. Then he reached into his bag and took out a huge, double-edged knife. The glint of it flashed before their eyes as he set about sharpening it with a stone. Thomossene and Suplera began to feel increasingly uncomfortable but Campira knew the knife was one of the key tools of the warlock's trade, used for carving tattoos and giving vaccinations, as well as for cutting up food.

'Right,' he said, once he deemed the blade sharp enough and the potion cool enough, 'Campira, take the woman outside and wait.'

The healer and Suplera stood up and made for the door, leaving Thomossene alone with the warlock.

'Take your clothes off!'

'Sorry?!' said Thomossene.

'I said take your clothes off, man!' said Phanga, brandishing the knife menacingly in his hands.

Thomossene complied, nervously eying the blade.

'Now lie down on your stomach!'

Again, Thomossene did as he was told, albeit slowly. Phanga sat down on his back, straddling him like a horse, and proceeded to cut a series of patterns into his skin. Thomossene's back quickly filled with blood but then Phanga took a greyish powder from his pouch and dabbed it into his wounds. The powder soaked up the blood but made Thomossene scream with pain. Indeed the pain was so great that for a moment he thought about begging for Phanga to stop and giving the whole thing up.

But then the desire to see his daughter came back into focus and he grit his teeth. After all, had he not already endured worse? The cuts on his back stung like crazy, but had he not already faced down a being known as N'tchira who no man had ever seen before? Had he not already had his back lacerated by the man now scarring tattoos into his skin? He'd done these things in the hope of getting Tchanaze back and now was not the time to give up and see those efforts go to waste. He and his wife had agreed to follow this thing through to the finish and that was what they would do.

The warlock went on covering the wounds with the powder, a substance of unknown provenance that turned black upon contact with Thomossene's blood. When all the tattoos were covered, Phanga went over to the fire and picked up the pot. He then bathed Thomossene from head to toe. The water was warm but infused with sedge grass, which made the cuts sting. Thomossene screamed out again in pain. Then Phanga had him roll over onto his back and finished the treatment by washing his torso.

'Get up and get dressed!' the warlock said. Thomossene did so with tears pouring from his eyes. 'Go outside and send your wife in!'

Thomossene went out and Suplera came in. 'Undress!' snapped Phanga.

'Excuse me?' she asked, surprised and scared at the sight

of the warlock's bloody knife. But the way Phanga looked back at her made it clear the matter was not up for debate. She began to remove her clothes and soon found herself standing naked before a man she believed to be the devil incarnate. He looked blankly at her bare body but she felt no shame, for it was the body that had produced Tchanaze, the most beautiful maiden in over a century of harvests.

'Lie on your stomach!' said Phanga and she complied. Just as he'd done with Thomossene, Phanga sat on her back, and without even wiping the blade clean, began carving symbols into her skin. Each incision drew a yelp from Suplera until the accumulation of pain had her wailing. Then the warlock began dousing her wounds with the powder and the pain grew worse, a burning sensation that was almost unbearable. But, like her husband, she blocked it out for she would sacrifice anything, including herself, for the child she'd borne.

'Stop crying, woman, you will soon cease to feel pain!' said Phanga, his voice calm, his face blank. 'There. Now get dressed!'

She picked herself up off the floor and started to dress. Tears ran down her face onto her breasts and beads, then dripped on the mat where they joined pools of blood, plant humus and human fragments. The whole mess gave off a dreadful, indecipherable smell as it trickled towards the door.

The warlock called the men back in and handed one a hoe and the other a broom.

'Sweep this up and bury it!' he said. 'We will be waiting for you outside!'

Thomossene and Campira cleaned up the hut until there was no trace left of the ritual that had just been performed. The healer was happy to assist, he did not feel that this kind of work was beneath him. Such tasks were usually left to an apprentice but he knew that the warlock was special, that dealing with him required patience and doing anything for him, no matter how menial, was an apprenticeship of sorts.

'We're all done, great master!' he said when he and Thomossene had finished.

'Very good,' said Phanga. 'Now follow me! It's time to check on Tchanaze, let's go and see N'tchimica!'

They set off following Phanga through the reeds, walking in single file. Thomossene and Suplera were feeling energised at the prospect of seeing Tchanaze, if not perhaps N'tchimica. Phanga had no relatives in Kumalolo but he did have friends, people who were in the same state as him and the same line of work. Dead people, in other words, who had escaped the dungeons of the underworld and come to Kumalolo to live in another person's skin and practise witchcraft. The couple's eagerness to see their daughter was therefore tempered by the prospect of meeting anyone the warlock might call a friend.

They walked for several hours, heading towards the setting sun and following the banks of the Zambeze. Phanga had expressly forbidden them from responding to anyone who greeted them on the way, for apparently only those who had not spoken to anyone during the journey would be admitted to wherever they were going. Thomossene and Suplera's backs began to ache, not with pain from their scars but from tiredness and the heat. It was the middle of the afternoon and the sun poured its heaviest rays down on them. By the time they came upon a rudimentary structure covered in sedge, they were dripping with sweat, their mouths dry with the taste of salt and blood.

The hut was located right on the riverbank. Small waves moved across the water, generated by the wind, and the reeds ruffled, but otherwise the world was still. The only living sound came from animals downstream craving food, ideally in the form of the human drowned.

Phanga went over to the hut and knocked on the door but got no answer. He tried again, then peered through a crack in the wall. But there was no one there, the place was empty. 'There's no one in!' he said, and for the first time ever they saw doubt cross his face.

He'd told them that he'd taken Tchanaze to the hut a few days ago. According to the conventions of witchcraft, certain aspects of the treatment the girl needed had to be performed by someone other than him. He had therefore sought the assistance of a colleague, N'tchimica, who had assured him that the girl would be back to full health by today. Phanga had clearly not expected the house to be empty.

'It doesn't look like anyone's been here for a while,' said Campira, after peering into the hut and inspecting the grounds. 'There's no sign of recent activity.'

'You're right,' said Phanga. 'They are not here.'

'Now what are we going to do?' Suplera asked, unable to hide her distress. Something unforeseen had obviously happened and she worried it might mean their daughter was gone for good.

'Do not worry, woman!' the warlock said. 'You and your daughter will be back in Sena by the end of the day or my name's not Phanga!'

He said this with such force that it made Suplera shudder.

Thomossene, too, noticed the warlock's change of tone, the sudden show of conviction.

'He's right,' said Campira. 'You mustn't worry!' He'd spoken firmly too but with more of a sense of compassion.

'We'll wait,' said the warlock, 'N'tchimica will be here in no time at all, I'm sure!'

The issue wasn't up for discussion, so they waited. And he was not wrong. A figure soon emerged from a nearby thicket and began walking towards them.

'It's him!' Phanga said, and despite his earlier assurances, they saw him breathe a sigh of relief.

As the figure got closer, they were better able to make him out. He was very short, though not as short as a *mwuanapatche*, and walked hunched over revealing a hump on his back. His right leg dragged, kicking up a cloud of dust, and he appeared to be extremely old. His hair was totally white and when he got near enough for them to see his face, they realised that the white hair on top of his head extended all the way down his cheeks in a sort of beard that covered his eyes and nose as well as his mouth.

'That's him alright!' said the warlock and he set off towards him. The two witches did not appear to exchange pleasantries when they met, they simply took each other by the arm and went straight into the hut. Campira, Thomossene and Suplera were left standing outside feeling a little confounded. They had not expected N'tchimica to be a man so old he could barely stand up. They knew that he was Phanga's friend and assumed that, like the warlock, he was a fugitive from hell who'd possessed another dead man's body. But what they couldn't understand was why he had chosen such a frail body when the Zambeze swallowed plenty of hearty young men and women each year.

After a short while the warlock appeared at the door to the hut and called the others in. There was a zebra skin spread out on the floor for them and Phanga and N'tchimica sat across from it on three-legged stools. They were smoking, passing a rolled-up tobacco leaf back and forth between them. Phanga took two big drags and exhaled, filling the room with thick, acrid smoke.

'Meet my good friend N'tchimica' he said, before adopting a very serious expression. 'Now I advise you to listen very carefully and do exactly what she tells you!'

The others looked at one another confused. Why had Phanga just called the old man a she?

'Why act so surprised, my children?' said the person in question. 'It is I, Nhantete, friend of your great master, Phanga!'

The visitors from Sena sat there stunned, a combination of astonishment and fear. The person addressing them was an old man with a hump on his back but the voice that came out of his mouth belonged to a woman.

'But…!' said Suplera.

'Yes, Suplera, I'm a woman just like you! We have spoken before, remember?'

Campira gasped, amazed at the revelation. Suplera and Thomossene were just as startled, because even if they had spoken to her before, it had been through Phanga.

'When I was alive, I took possession of the belongings of a stranger who lived in Sena. I told you both this, if you recall? I contracted *n'fúcua* because of it, which as you know is a deadly disease. When I died, in one of the shipwrecks of the era, I passed the disease on to my daughter and when she died she passed it on to her granddaughter, a girl you all know,' Nhantete said. 'Mbemba!'

'What?' said Thomossene.

'Of course!' Campira exclaimed. 'That's why Farença and Mbemba have been skulking around!'

'As you know,' Nhantete continued calmly, 'Mbemba has always been plagued by *n'fúcua* and never courted by the young men of Sena. As you also know, Tchanaze, your daughter, was the apple of every man's eye, from Sena to Mutarara, Chupanga, Chinde and Muanza. So Mbemba arranged for her *n'fúcua* to be transferred into Tchanaze and the disease claimed your daughter's life!'

'What do you mean?' asked Suplera in a panic. 'Are you saying that woman from Inhangoma is not our daughter?'

'That is not what I said,' countered Nhantete.

They all fell silent while they gathered their thoughts.

'What should we do now?' Campira eventually offered.

'Nothing,' said Nhantete. 'Or rather Phanga will tell you what to do in a moment. He asked me to inhabit this body in order to help you, and that is why I am here, because he is a very dear friend! You have no idea how fond of one another we are.'

'Indeed Nhantete and I know each other extremely well,' Phanga said, standing up and pointing to the door. 'You can believe us when we say you will have your daughter back soon!'

The warlock led them outside before going back in to confer with Nhantete again. He then reappeared and gestured for them to follow him, striking out into the bush in the direction N'tchimica had come from. They walked further and further into the undergrowth until they came upon two holes in the ground. Each contained a kind of jar or tub, just about wide enough for a human to fit in and deep enough for them to stand upright. Next to each hole was a basin.

'You see those basins?' said Phanga.

'Yes,' replied Campira, speaking for the others but just as bewildered as them.

'Thomossene, you and your wife take those basins and bring back water from the river until the jars are full. Campira, you make a small fire beside them. I will wait in the hut until you're finished!'

The warlock left and Thomossene and Suplera set off for the river with the basins. Campira set about gathering wood and by the time the couple had got back with their first load, he had the fire going. The sun above made its way west, seeking a place to rest for the night, and migratory birds flew around doing likewise. Thomossene and Suplera went back and forth to the river and the jars gradually filled. Campira's fire grew in intensity and the reflection of the flames in the water made a rainbow.

'That'll do!' said Campira, much to the exhausted couple's relief. 'I'll go and get Phanga.'

The healer came back a few minutes later with Phanga and N'tchimica, the mysterious couple, friends or lovers from Satan's land. They inspected the jars and saw that they were brimful and that the water was clear, for the river at that time of year did not carry the detritus of huts and crops destroyed by floods or the body parts of the drowned.

Phanga and N'tchimica, or Nhantete, had brought bags with them. They each knelt down beside one of the jars, took a purple powder out of their bag and sprinkled the substance into the water. The powder quickly dissolved and turned the water blood red. It even smelled of blood and Thomossene and Suplera took this as yet another sign of the witches' otherworldly powers. The two fugitives from hell then stood up and walked back to the hut, without so much as saying a word. Even Campira appeared surprised by this but then Phanga turned around and summoned him. Campira headed over to the hut and Thomossene and Suplera realised something that Campira had always known: Phanga did not in any way consider the healer to be his peer. How could it be otherwise given that Campira had never died?

He wasn't gone for long. Thomossene and Suplera watched the healer walk back towards them through the undergrowth and they tried to read the look on his face.

'Right, my friends, we'll set off back to Sena at dawn,' he said.

'But what about Tchanaze?' said Thomossene.

'Don't worry about her. Phanga knows what he's doing!' Campira said. 'He will meet us in Sena and bring Tchanaze with him. She'll be back to her old self and fully cured of *n'fúcua*.'

'But...' said Thomossene uncertainly. He had many doubts but expressed perhaps the least of them: 'He doesn't even know where we live!'

'Look, Thomossene, do not ever doubt Phanga,' the healer said rather brusquely. 'He has powers of a kind never before seen!'

Thomossene said no more after that. He looked at his wife and she too remained silent, for there was no denying the warlock's powers were terrifying.

'Now listen carefully to what I am about to tell you,' said Campira. 'Take off your clothes and get into the jars. Don't come out until the liquid has fully congealed.'

The couple began to strip and the healer went back to see his master in the hut. Night cast its mystical colours over the bush and the stars began to fill the firmament over Kumalolo. Thomossene and Suplera lowered themselves into the jars and when Campira came back he found them both up to their necks in the liquid, which looked like blood and was slowly thickening.

'Very good,' said the healer, 'that's exactly it!' But he saw no sign of satisfaction on their faces, just the resigned, slightly bitter look of people who knew their lives were beholden to the capricious whims of river spirits.

'The master said you are to stick your heads under when I give the signal,' said Campira. He had brought a bowl with him containing a sort of cassava flour made from tubers that grew in the Zambeze riverbed.

'Now!' he said, and Thomossene and Suplera duly dipped their heads under. But only for a fraction of a second because the liquid was impossibly unpleasant. 'Again!' yelled Campira before they'd even had a chance to catch their breathe. And on it went for several minutes until it became unfeasible because the liquid, which was of unknown origin but resembled plasma, had completely curdled.

'Well done!' said Campira. 'Now I will turn my back and you can get out and dry yourselves!'

He turned around and the couple hoisted themselves up and out of the jars. They wiped themselves down with a cloth, trying to remove red stains and bits of congealed blood from their skin.

'Now rub that flour all over you!' said Campira, still looking the other way.

The couple picked up the bowl and rubbed the powder into their skin. Pain shot through their bodies wherever the powder came into contact with the tattoos the warlock had cut into them.

'We are done!' said Suplera, touching the worst of her wounds gently with her fingers and wincing with pain. 'Now what?'

'Get dressed,' the healer said. 'We'll rest here until dawn.'

'What about Phanga and his friend?'

'Look, Thomossene, forget about Phanga,' Campira urged. 'He wishes us a safe journey and he'll see us in Sena. Now try to get some sleep. Tomorrow is going to be a big day!'

XIX

PHANGA SURPASSES HIMSELF

Morning had long since crept over the horizon and the sun risen high in the sky, sending its fierce rays down on the houses below. The rooftops spread from the banks of the Zambeze out across the plains and towards the foothills, for this was Sena, where the mountains sought to strangle the river. It was a land where mysteries arose from the water's depths for spirits lived there, the souls of generations of men and women who'd perished in currents that ran from Mutarara to Caia and all the way down to Chinde and the Indian Ocean.

But the latest mystery had people more dumfounded than usual because everyone, absolutely everyone, had born witness to Tchanaze's demise. Child of Thomossene and Suplera, daughter to all, sweetheart to every man, Tchanaze was the pride and joy of the whole valley. Anyone who saw her fell instantly in love and many who'd never laid eyes on her did too, for mere tell of her charms was enough to render most men smitten. There wasn't a man alive who didn't dream of breathing in the perfume of her breasts and touching the glow of her tattooed skin, and because you didn't have to be alive to dream, the dead craved her too and discussed her beauty from the Zambeze's sandbanks to the graveyard clay.

Everyone knew that Tchanaze had died and everyone knew that she'd died from *n'fúcua*. But what no one could explain was how she'd contracted the demonic disease in the fist place, for she'd always been a hale and hearty girl and none of the menfolk had ever detected *n'fúcua* in her. Everyone had attended her burial and sensed the bacchanal presence of evil spirits, and everyone had attended her unburial and recoiled upon seeing a dead cat where her corpse should have lain. Evil spirits were clearly manifesting and word soon drifted across the river that Tchanaze was alive and living in the reeds of Inhangoma. Her parents had gone to find her, accompanied by the healer, and then they'd gone to Kumalolo, and then they'd gone to Gorongoza, and still nobody would say anything about it.

For these reasons and more, when Thomossene, Suplera and Campira got back to Sena that day, they found a village in turmoil. People had abandoned their tasks in the fields, left tools to lie wherever they fell and rushed out of homes without shutting their doors. They were all running in one direction, which was the same direction Thomossene, Suplera and Campira were heading in, so they fell in with the crowd and became part of the flow. Some people looked at them with a sense of awe but, unlike on recent occasions, nobody asked them any questions. Yet the more they walked, the more it became apparent where everyone was going: Thomossene and Suplera's house.

By the time the couple reached their own home, a huge crowd had assembled in front of it, to the side of it and even in the yard behind it. The whole village appeared to be there, but it wasn't just people from Sena, people had come across the bridge at Mutarara and from as far away as Assena and Massena. There were so many people that Thomossene and Suplera couldn't get anywhere near their front door. Campira took charge and elbowed his way through the crowd, dragging Thomossene and Suplera with him. As people stepped aside, a circle formed around them, which slowly began to change into another, larger circle, a clearing that hadn't been visible to them when they'd first arrived. At the centre of this clearing was a mat and on it sat two people. Thomossene and Suplera's jaws dropped when they saw who they were.

The rearrangement of the crowd had allowed more people to get a glimpse of the two figures and there was a collective intake of breath. The first figure was a man with a bony face and a skeletal body covered in strange tattoos and necklaces and beads that reflected not the sun but a light of unknown providence. The scowl on his face and the ferocity of his stare were unlike anything anyone present had ever seen, regardless of whether they'd come from Sena, Mutarara, Caia or Chupanga.

The second figure was a woman of rare beauty whose

beads were so enchanting the crowd became instantly drunk with love. Her body was sculptural, the curves of her hips were marked, and any man who witnessed her smile felt his heart skip a beat. It was Tchanaze. Her beauty, her charm, her very presence left people stunned and ecstatic and tears welled in people's eyes, tears of joy and tears of perplexity, because they knew the woman before them had died.

'Mum! Dad!' yelled Tchanaze when she saw her parents pushing through the throng. She jumped up and the crowd dispersed enough for Suplera to rush forward and embrace her daughter. Tears poured down their cheeks as they hugged and kissed, and Thomossene made it through too and there was a further outpouring of joy. Soon the whole crowd was crying, letting their emotions out like they hadn't done for a long time. No one who witnessed the scene would forget it and word of it would reach every corner of the land.

Farença and Mbemba were among those who witnessed it, of course. They found themselves standing right at the front of the cordon, utterly disorientated, unsure of what to do or how best to react to events. These developments met neither with their own expectations nor Nhahana's instructions. Three days she'd told them to wait before going back to see Mabureza, three days when only two had passed. Anger and frustration inevitably began to rise in Mbemba's chest because none of this was supposed to happen and here was her hated rival besides, a woman who was supposed to be dead but who was standing right there before her, flaunting her very existence and dazzling everyone with her beauty. How was it possible? Hadn't she died of *n'fúcua*?

These questions tormented Mbemba's mind and others

pondered them too. It had to be the good spirits' doing, people said, they'd used Tchanaze to announce bountiful crops of sorghum and pearl millet and so they'd brought her back to carry on doing so.

'Tchanaze, my dear child! Tchanaze, my dear child!' Suplera cried over and over again, hugging the girl and stroking her braids, as every male present longed to do.

'Óh Tchanaze! How wonderful it is to have you back!' said Thomossene, amazed to see his daughter behaving like her old self and amazed to see her at all, because they'd rushed back from Kumalolo by the quickest route possible themselves and yet she'd beaten them to it.

The whole crowd seemed to share in his amazement and a round of applause spontaneously broke out. Cheers of joy and jubilation followed and then suddenly the sound of drums filled the air and people started dancing, moving in and out of the circle to caress Tchanaze, the fairest maiden of them all.

The gathering had turned into a party but one man remained impervious to it all: Phanga. He remained right where he was, sitting on the mat, an absent look on his face. Taken by the beat of the drum, people had forgotten he was even there let alone how frightening he was. Billets of *cabanga* appeared and were passed around and everyone drank and became merry. Everyone except Phanga, and except Farença and Mbemba too, for they were feeling increasingly uncomfortable. They could not share in the sense of celebration and yet they could not very easily remove themselves either. But then the fervour went up a notch because Suplera and Tchanaze entered what had become an improvised dance floor and whirled one another around to woops of delight.

Farença and Mbemba took the opportunity to slip away, their heads bowed, their chests burning with hatred and grievance. They felt betrayed. They'd walked back and forth to Kumalolo and been told to return again in three days. But now what were they supposed to do? Oughtn't they to go back right away and find Nhahana? Or was there no point because it was too soon and Mabureza wouldn't be there yet?

A witch's instructions had to be obeyed to the letter and that meant letting events unfold as the spirits wished them too. Those events had taken an unexpected turn but Nhahana had told them to trust in Mabureza, that he would never abandon them.

But did they trust in Mabureza? Did they trust Nhahana? It was hard to trust someone when they were inside another person's body. Of course, witches drew their wisdom and power from being both alive and dead, from being able to access the combined knowledge of the drowned of every generation. But if you couldn't be sure who you were talking to how could you know if they were being honest with you or had your best interests at heart? Nhahana's voice wasn't even clearly that of a man or a woman, indeed at times she'd reminded Farença of Mabureza. Hadn't they worn the same necklace too?

Meanwhile, the celebration continued and Phanga remained where he was, inside the party but outside the exultation. People had forgotten he was sitting there and so it came as a shock when he slowly got to his feet and spoke in a voice that was croaky but loud enough to be heard above the din: 'Women, children and men of Sena, listen to me!'

It was as if a king had addressed his subjects because the

drummers immediately stopped drumming and the dancers froze. Absorbed in the moment they may have been, but his voice was so authoritative it sent shivers down their spines and everyone now turned to face the warlock as he walked over to join Thomossene, Suplera and Tchanaze in the centre of the circle. The silence was funereal, the crowd hypnotised by the fearsome witch with the bony frame and the blank expression.

'I have come here to return to you the woman who filled your hearts with fire and your souls with moonlight!' he said and then he paused to allow for an ovation. 'To bring back the fair maiden who had every young man in Sena consumed with passion and all the menfolk from here to Cheringoma besides!' Again he let cheers and applause ring out and die down before he continued. 'People of Sena, before I go on, I would like Mbemba and her mother to come and stand here with me!'

This time his words were met with shrugs of surprise. This was not what they'd expected to hear and they couldn't understand why he'd mentioned the two women or wanted them beside him.

'They're not here!' someone shouted from the back. 'They just left!'

'Then go and get them!' cried Phanga. 'Bring them back here whether they like it or not!'

A group of volunteers ran off in the direction of Farença and Mbemba's house. They found the two women shuffling along with tears in their eyes.

'Come with us!' said one of the volunteers, infusing his voice with Phanga's authority.

'Why?' said Mbemba.

'That witch from Kumalolo wants to see you!'

The words cut through Farença and Mbemba's souls like glass.

'No!' Farença said. 'We're not going anywhere!' But she broke down crying as she said it. She didn't know what the man wanted but if he was a witch from Kumalolo he presumably knew what they'd done.

The search party marched the two women back to where the crowd was gathered and pushed them into the circle. Phanga stood waiting, arms folded, an impenetrable expression on his face. Farença and Mbemba fell at his feet.

'Men and women of Sena! These people here,' he pointed a skeletal finger at first Mbema and then Farença, 'transmitted the *n'fúcua* into Tchanaze!'

The crowd gasped.

'They destroyed the love of your lives out of pure jealousy! They could not accept that Tchanaze was the object of every young man's affections, that her skin glowed, her beads dazzled and her beauty enchanted, while Mbemba, ugly and plain, turned no man's head.'

'That's true,' the crowd muttered. 'There's no comparison.'

'As you know, Mbemba suffered from *n'fúcua*. She inherited the condition from her maternal great grandmother, a woman named Nhantete who contracted the disease after taking possession of the belongings of a dead person here in Sena!'

A murmur rippled through the crowd as people took in Phanga's revelations and watched Farença and Mbemba squirm at his feet.

'I know this because Nhantete and I are intimates and I know that these two women went to Kumalolo and consulted a witch there, a nobody, an upstart who on their instruction cast a spell on Tchanaze, a spell that they knew would lead to her isolation and certain death. Is that not so?' he bellowed, turning to Mbemba and Farença.

'No!' they cried in unison, tears pouring down their faces.

'We'll soon see about that,' said Phanga. 'This witch they commissioned thought he was very clever but he made a mistake in choosing the skeleton he did, for it belonged to a friend of the man whose body stands before you now and the spirits of that man and that skeleton visited Tchanaze in her death throes and were left besotted. That's right, people, because just as your menfolk worshipped Tchanaze so too did the spirits of your ancestors drink in the intoxicating aroma of her moonlit skin. They decided to save her and so a cat was buried in her stead in order to fool you. A tug of war broke out in the spirit world, won by the spirits of bumper corn harvests and three shipwrecked friends, and it is on behalf of those spirits, and as the living embodiment of one of those friends, that I present you with Tchanaze here today, as beautiful and alive as ever!'

The crowd erupted in raucous applause.

'What are we going to do with the two little she-devils then?' someone shouted, causing heads to turn towards Farença and Mbemba.

'Men and women of Sena,' said Phanga, 'let me, in the presence of you, ask these two women the following: is what I have just said true?'

Both women were sobbing so hard it looked like they might not be capable of speaking. But Mbemba found the strength to answer: 'It's not true!'

'And you Farença, what have you got to say for yourself?' asked Phanga.

'It's a lie, it's a lie!' she screamed, distraught and hysterical.

'Very well!' said Phanga. 'Women and men of this land, you will now see how your forebears judge those who seek to defy an ancestral curse and banish beauty from your midst!'

He took a flask from his pouch and held it up for everyone to see. It contained a dark green potion that looked unlike anything anyone present had ever seen before. Then he removed the lid and the crowd winced, for the stench of it was so strong it could be smelled in the rows right at the back.

'Bring me a dog!' Phanga shouted and a number of men rushed off to find a dog. There were lots of dogs in Sena, so it didn't take long.

'Here you go!' said a man bringing the witch a stray.

Phanga took the dog and held it by the scruff of the neck, the animal making not so much as a whimper. 'Watch while I give this dog a few drops of the liquid!' said the warlock.

Taking the flask in his left hand, he held the dog's mouth open with his right and let a few drops of the green potion drip onto the animal's tongue. Then he laid the dog down and let it go. The dog remained where it was, standing beside the witch looking a bit self-conscious. Phanga allowed a few minutes to pass then said: 'Has anything happened to the dog?'

'No!' roared the crowd, unsure of where the warlock was going with this.

'Now I need a volunteer,' he said, 'someone brave enough to drink a few drops.'

A man stepped forward. The witch instructed him to open

his mouth and then he let a few drops of potion fall on the man's tongue. Again Phanga waited a few minutes before saying anything.

'Has anything happened to this man?' he asked.

'No!' everyone cried, their curiosity building.

'Now pay attention!' said Phanga. 'I will give a few drops to Thomossene and his wife.'

He beckoned for the couple to come forward and open their mouths. He put a droplet or two on each of their tongues and stepped back to allow for the now customary wait.

'Has anything happened to them?' he said.

'No!' people yelled, beginning to grow a little impatient.

'Very good. One last question: Farença, did you and your daughter arrange for a spell to be cast on Tchanaze? Yes or no?'

He said this last bit in such a thunderous voice that it made the whole crowd shudder, never mind the woman being asked the question. Farença looked at her daughter, whose head was bowed, tears streaming down her face. Neither of them knew what to say for who could tell what special properties the potion contained? They'd arranged for a spell to be cast on Tchanaze, of course they had, they'd bid Mabureza do it. But where was Mabureza now? Farença was tempted to pray to him for a moment, to beg him to come to their rescue. But she knew he had abandoned them and gone into hiding, from them and from this man, this mighty witch, Thomossene and Suplera's witch.

Mbemba drew courage from somewhere and got to her feet. She stood there stiffly and seemed to be waiting for her mother to do the same, so Farença forced herself up. Mbemba stared the warlock in the face, and again Farença followed her lead. It looked like they might be about to confess and beg for forgiveness, but they did no such thing.

'No,' said Mbemba.

'We had nothing to do with any spell!' said Farença.

They had both spoken resolutely, determined to hide their fear from the audience.

'Very well. Then are you prepared to drink from this flask?' asked Phanga. 'Bear in mind that the potion will only act on those who lie!'

This last revelation made Farença almost choke. But what choice did they have? She noticed Mbemba give Tchanaze a hard stare before presenting Phanga with her open jaw. Farença looked at Thomossene and Suplera before doing the same.

'If that is your wish then so it will be done!' said Phanga and he poured several drops of the potion down their throats.

The liquid was tasteless at first, or at least its flavour was indecipherable. Then a burning sensation spread through their tongues, before shooting down their throats and into their stomachs. Their heads went dizzy and the weight of their bodies became too much for their legs to support. They fell to the ground, both of them at the same time, as if struck by lightning.

Phanga looked out upon the astonished crowd with a blank expression.

'Women and men, boys and girls of Sena! What you have just witnessed is the punishment your ancestors mete out to those who dare disturb their everlasting peace. The spirits presented you with a gift,' the warlock paused to look at Tchanaze, 'a maiden so fair she stirs passions in the living and the dead. Appreciate her, worship her beauty, and above all else never forget that she belongs to the underworld as well as to this world. Respect the spirits and those of us who straddle both worlds, have us cast spells when spells must be cast but be careful who you ask to cast them. I am Phanga and I have spoken. Now take these two bodies away and bury them!'

As soon as he'd finished speaking he started walking and a path opened in the crowd to let him through. He bid nobody farewell and nobody said goodbye to him. His steps were short and his progress was slow but he never looked back. He moved like a corpse shuffling through a graveyard after rising from a tomb.

Behind him lay the stricken bodies of Mbemba and Farença. Tchanaze stood over them, her eyes sparkling as she watched the warlock go, but her face was blank, almost sad. Thomossene and Suplera too watched Phanga depart with somewhat downcast expressions, their mouths not opening to offer any words of thanks or invitations to stay. Campira was the only one to offer anything resembling a smile. He'd enjoyed the warlock's performance and was pleased the matter had been resolved. He was also glad their paths had crossed for there was no doubt Phanga was the most powerful witch in the land.

Campira ordered his ministrants to take Mbemba and Farença's bodies away and bury them. But that was it, there would be no ceremony.

Then someone began to hum a song, which soon became a chant and gained a drumbeat. The party started up again. After all, one man's misfortune was another man's gain. The fearsome warlock disappeared from view and the villagers were able to forget about him. They danced and drank and celebrated the return of Tchanaze, the most beautiful woman in the land.

Dedalus Africa

Under the editorship of Jethro Soutar and Yovanka Perdigão, Dedalus Africa seeks out high-quality fiction from all of Africa, including parts of Africa hitherto totally ignored by English-language publishers. Titles currently available are:

The Desert and the Drum – Mbarek Ould Beyrouk
Catalogue of a Private Life – Najwa Bin Shatwan
The Word Tree – Teolinda Gersão
The Madwoman of Serrano – Dina Salústio
The Ultimate Tragedy – Abdulai Silá
Our Musseque – José Luandino Vieira
Co-wives, Co-widows – Adrienne Yabouza
Edo's Souls – Stella Gaitano
Tchanaze – Carlos Paradona Rufino Roque

Forthcoming titles include:

Saara – Mbarek Ould Beyrouk

For further details email: info@dedalusbooks.com